Colt O'Brien
Sees The Light

A Novel

By

George Matthew Cole

Young Colt O'Brien (Book 1)

Printed in the United States of America

First published by Dog Ear Publishing 2009
4010 W. 86th Street, Ste H
Indianapolis, IN 46268
www.dogearpublishing.net

ISBN-13: 978-1495372391
ISBN-10: 1495372391
Second Edition

This is a work of fiction. Names, characters, businesses, places, events and
incidents are either the products of the author's imagination or used in a
fictitious manner. Any resemblance to actual persons, living or dead, or
actual events is purely coincidental.

Original cover art by Terry Smith
Cover design by George Matthew Cole

Find more information about the author
and his books at his web site.

www.georgemcole.com

For those who remember the goal
in the midst of chaos.

RECOGNITION

I'm fortunate to belong to a special support
group made up of fellow writers. This group
was formed by individuals that attended a creative
writing class at Highline Community College in
Washington State. The teacher Marjorie Rommel
has a special talent for making adult students feel
at ease when exploring their writing potential. I
appreciate the support of the individuals listed
below. Without them the journey would have been
much longer and much lonelier.

Thanks to all

Jeanette
Jolanda
Marilyn
Marjorie
Rob
Sandi
Susan
Vera
Wendy

Colt O'Brien
Sees The Light

Chapter 1

------Email-------
From: O'Brien, Colt[ColtOB@yahoo.com]
To: Jones, Bobby[bobbyj@yahoo.com]
Subject: Wow Computers
Sent: Sun 10/16/1994

Yo
pcs r great   am getting how they work
we can start fixing them and make bucks
am done with sprts man   Dude   I stopped
growing $%#$$@$%%^
 later

------Email-------

Puddles of brown water pockmarked the soccer field
reflecting the bright midday sun. The recently ended downpour
had cleansed the air and the earth, leaving everything smelling
fresh and pure. A large pond, about six inches deep, covered
much of the center of the field. Parents, brothers, sisters and
friends yelled encouragement as two teams of thirteen-year-old
boys slogged up, down and across the swampy play area. All of
the on-watchers still wore ponchos, coats and other rain gear,
even though the skies were clear. In the Pacific Northwest, a
sunny sky did not guarantee that rain would stay away for long.
The crimson and green, once shiny, uniforms of the respective
teams were soaked and muddied. The players had difficulty
handling the round white and black ball in the sloppy conditions.
Flying mud and water slowed the players as each tried to gain an

1

advantage. Neither team was able to control the ball for a substantial length time. Mud holes, slipperiness and the dreaded pond, created formidable barriers to forward progress. Goalies at each end of the field gazed off into the distance waiting for something to happen. It was near half-time and not one shot on goal had been attempted.

Once again, the elusive soccer ball was floating in the middle of the pond, daring any player to slap, splash, kick or cajole it onto solid ground. A tall lanky boy on the green team splashed through the water toward the soaked, leather globe. With great effort he kicked the ball out of the pond toward the sideline. Water splashed up, swirling around, as it floated toward solid ground. The ball seemed to be made out of lead and landed with a thud. Another player received the pass and waited. He looked downfield for an opening as the players on the crimson team slogged toward him.

He yelled, "Atta way, Eric. Good kick."

With legs thrashing and water flying, the now excited Eric lunged forward toward the edge of the pond.

"Pass it to me. I'm open," he cried.

The ball was waiting for Eric when he broke out of the expanse of water. He arrived just ahead of four opponents. The stork-like player methodically dribbled up the sideline. He managed to avoid the potholes and puddles, allowing him to speed past mid-field. Fans on both sidelines were surprised that any player had broken away from the pack. They started yelling words of encouragement to their prospective teams. The energized green team saw their first real chance to take a shot. Boys on the crimson team scrambled to recover and stop the tall boy's aggressive attack. As his team attempted to adjust to this new situation, a small player wearing crimson, shot away from his teammates like a bullet in flight. The mud covering most of his body could not hide fierce, dark blue eyes beneath a head of jet black hair. He ran after the much taller Eric who was weaving past players on both teams on his way to the goal. All other players on the field seemed to be merely walking as he loped like a miniature gazelle toward the taller adversary.

From the sideline, a pretty, blonde teenage girl yelled, "Tackle, Colt, tackle the ball!"

Colt met Eric as he was circling toward the goal where the now, wide-awake goalie was bracing for an onslaught. Colt's legs moved like powerful miniature pistons. They pummeled the ball and the taller boy's legs at the same time. After a furious, but futile, attempt to ward off his attacker, Eric lost his footing. He fell forward face down, onto the muddy ground as the ball skipped out of bounds. Eric jumped up spitting and shaking his head. His face was covered with mud. There was thick, wet dirt in his eyes and mouth. He glared at the referee and yelled.

"That was a foul ref, call it!"

"He went for the ball. No foul. Play on." replied the referee without making eye contact with the angry player.

Eric looked at Colt and spoke.

"Watch out, you little midget. It's coming. You won't know when, but it's coming."

"Bring it on, stork boy. You'll end up in the same place, eating mud."

Colt walked toward Eric with a determined stare. His fists were clenched, ready for battle. The shrill sound of the whistle stopped him.

"Half time," yelled the referee.

The tired boys walked to the sidelines where orange wedges and Gatorade were waiting. Colt O'Brien approached his sister, Kelly, and his father, Robert. Kelly, athletic, trim and blonde, was about the same height as Colt. Her pale blue eyes were a few shades lighter than her brother's. For a fourteen-year-old girl, she exuded noticeable confidence. She put her arm around Colt and smiled.

"Did you hear me out there, Colt?" she asked.

"Yeah, I heard 'tackle the ball'," he answered.

"Good tackle. That's the way I'd do it,"

"Could you believe that guy was flipping me crap?" said Colt with a flash of anger in his eyes.

"He didn't like the Colt treatment. He went swimming," laughed Kelly.

Colt smiled and started eating orange wedges.

Colt's father, Robert, was tall, dark and commanding. His gray, perceptive eyes, displayed fearless control and a competitive nature. Specks of gray ran throughout his full head of dark hair. He carried himself like a man who was accustomed to being followed and respected. He looked at Colt with an even stare.

Colt looked back at his father. *Man, I can't tell if he liked what I did or not. What the hell? It seems like I never know anymore,* he thought.

"That kid was big, but you can take him. I'll bet he's used to getting his way. Don't let him push you around." said Robert.

Colt raised his chin with clenched jaw.

"Don't worry about that, Dad. You saw how I handled him."

Crap, he acts like I didn't do anything. I stopped the goal and it's like it never happened. What does it take?

Soon the whistle blew and the second half began. Play continued, with neither team gaining an advantage or scoring a goal. A few minutes remained in the game when the ball was passed to Colt near mid-field. He skillfully ran around the pond, avoiding defenders, as he loped toward the goal. After using fancy footwork to keep the ball away from an opposing player, Colt focused his attention toward the goal. As he increased speed, the short, feisty boy was startled by something flashing in front of his eyes. He tried to duck, but was hit by an elbow on his right cheekbone causing a crack to ring out. The excruciating pain caused him to see swirling red and white, sparkling stars. The crowd groaned as Colt fell to the ground. For a few seconds he lay still. After shaking his head, he jumped up enraged, and sprinted toward his attacker. When he saw that it was Eric, who waited with a smirk on his face, he became even more agitated. When Colt was close to Eric, he began swinging both arms. The taller boy easily pushed him away while laughing and taunting. Colt continued to swing his arms like a perpetual motion machine, but was not able to hit his target. His frustration grew as Eric repelled him with ease.

The referee stepped between the two boys, pushing them apart. He pulled a red card from his uniform and said, "You're out of the game, green. Get moving, now!"

Eric smiled at Colt, who was holding a hand to his sore face.

"Who's the punk now? You're such a shrimp that you couldn't get near me."

Colt lunged at Eric, but was grabbed and held back by strong arms. He looked up as Eric ambled away. Colt was relieved to see that his father was there to support him. Then, he was overcome with a deep dark sadness. As he looked into his father's eyes, it was as if a window had opened that allowed the thirteen-year-old boy to look into his father's mind. There he saw and felt the thoughts that he feared more than anything in life. Colt sensed his disappointment behind those eyes. He knew that his father wanted more from him. No audible words were needed for the boy to understand. Colt flailed away in frustrated sadness until he was free of his father's arms.

5

Through his tears, he looked at his father and spoke.

"You don't care about me. You just care that I'm not big and tall. Well, maybe it's not something I can do anything about."

"But, but…," said Robert.

"Leave me alone. I'm quitting sports forever. I'll never win," said Colt as he walked away.

Chapter 2

------Email-------
From: O'Brien, Robert[ROBrian@aol.com]
To: Norman, Ted[TNorman@yahoo.com]
Subject: Colt

Hello Ted
You asked how my son Colt is doing. I guess we can discuss this in person, but the short version is that he is not doing well. He was a great athlete but now he is only average. I'm sure you can see why I would be disappointed. I can't understand why his sister keeps getting better at soccer and Colt doesn't. Hell, I'm six feet three inches. He should be taller and bigger than he is. I'm starting to think he is using his short stature as an excuse for not performing. I think you know that I won't tolerate that.

Let's talk soon.
Bob

------Email-------

Colt O'Brien sat in his bedroom wearing his soggy, soccer uniform. He looked out the window, with glazed eyes, at tiny gentle, raindrops showering down. As if in a trance he stared, trying to block out a continuous stream of images flashing across his inner vision. He saw scenes of soccer, the face of his father, his sister, and most of all a crowd of faceless, zombie-like fans. All of the scenes were colored by a mixture of frustration, anger and a heavy feeling of utter defeat. *I'm sick of feeling like I'm a loser even if I do okay. I know I can be good at something. I'll show him that I can be the best, even if it isn't in sports. I can't help it if every guy is passing me up.*

After a knock on the door, Colt said in a loud voice, "Nobody's home."

"Honey, let me in. I know you had a bad day. I heard you slam the door," said his mother, Leona.

Colt smiled and, for a moment, his dark face brightened. *At least it's not the old man*, he thought. After plopping down on the soaking wet chair, Colt looked at his mother. She was petite with short blond hair and bright green eyes that were accented by worry wrinkles. Her appearance was one of manicured elegance reflected in her subtle makeup and expensive apparel. It was obvious to Colt that she was concerned about him which started to nudge him out of his emotional quagmire. *Here's one person who really loves me.*

Leona cringed and picked at his wet uniform.

"Oh honey, you're soaking wet. You need to get out of those wet clothes and warm up."

The boy stared at his mother with dark blue eyes that darted from side to side. His lower lip quivered.

"I've been thinking, thinking a lot," said Colt.

"Honey, I know you think your Dad is disappointed in you, but he just wants you to be happy," said Leona, trying to be convincing.

Colt's angry eyes stopped darting and peered directly at her. She stepped back a little to adjust to the glare of anguish coming at her. She hesitated trying to center herself and focus before speaking. Colt responded to her.

"You know I can tell stuff. I know what he's thinking. He doesn't care about me. He just wants to brag to his friends that I can win at sports," said Colt.

"But honey, he's your father. He loves you, just like I do."

"Nobody loves me like you do, Mom," he said with a quick smile.

"Listen to me, Colt. You've always had what my grandmother would call the gift. I know you can feel and see things that other people can't. It worries me that people won't understand your special talent. Are you still having those weird dreams?"

Colt was now moving in another direction as his inner life came into the foreground. This was something that was his alone. It made him special.

"Yeah, I still have the dream where I see fog in front of the sun. In my dream I try to get past the fog into the sunlight, but I never can," said Colt.

"Let's keep this between ourselves. You may not know this, but very few people can do what you do. Your father definitely would not understand. Don't give people reasons to think you're not like they are."

"Don't worry. No way I'm having my friends think I'm a crazy dude." answered Colt.

Leona smiled as she sensed that the love of her life was starting to regain his positive outlook.

"That's settled then. Kelly said you did fine in the game but a mean boy knocked you down. There will be other games."

Colt looked up at his loving mother and felt the full force of her love but knew that his life was about to change. *I won't tell her now, but I've had it with sports. Kelly can be the star. She won't disappoint Dad.*

~~~

Colt sat at a table in the cafeteria of Sylvester Junior High. He looked around the crowded room for his friend, Bobby Jones. He spotted the lanky boy and waved him over.

"Dude, sit down and listen. I've got great news." said an enthusiastic Colt.

Bobby paused after sitting down. A quizzical expression flitted across his face.

"Hi Colt. What's goin' on?" he replied.

"I got us jobs doin' the computer thing. It'll be fantastic."

Bobby Jones had distinct brown eyes with light brown hair. He was thin, but not skinny. At hearing Colt's idea, his eyes became wide and he looked up in frustration. His hands tightened, reflecting the tension in the rest of his body.

"Er, uh, what thing? Man, here we go again. What did you volunteer me for?" said Bobby with a bit of frustration.

Colt could hardly stay seated through his excitement. He smiled with a conspiratorial confidence. His enthusiasm was flowing like a deep river directly at his friend.

"The computer tech thing, dude. We'll be fixing computers and stuff," said Colt.

Bobby looked around nervously.

"But, but, I don't know that much and you don't either," he said.

"Hey, we both have computers and I know one of the tech guys. He'll help us. Hell, half the time you just reboot'em anyway."

"They let seventh graders do that?" asked Bobby in a high-pitched whine.

Now, Colt could see that his friend was not as confident as he was. *Damn, I need to convince him. He's getting wimpy on me as usual.* After a few moments of attempting to sense Bobby's state of mind, Colt was ready to continue. *Now I know what to say.*

"Listen! If we do this we get an automatic "A" in a class. Also, we help teachers with problems. That has to be good.

You know how you like getting in good with teachers," said Colt.

The pale, shy boy relaxed a little allowing some of the tension to release from his body.

"Keep talking. I'm listening," he said.

Colt saw his window of opportunity and moved in for the finish.

"Dude, dude, we can make money on the side instead of some dead-end job flippin' burgers or whatever. We can do this. I know we can."

"I'll probably regret this, but okay. I wonder if I should ever listen to you."

Colt jumped up, thrusting both arms into the air, and yelled "Yes."

Chapter 3

------Email-------
From: O'Brien, Kelly[Kellyobrien@aol.org]
To: Todd, Brianna[BriannaT@yahoo.com]
Subject: Colt

Hi Bri
Wow!!!! My little brother is getting a lot of attention from the babes. They are coming up to me all giggly and shy asking if he has a girlfriend. Don't get me wrong, I love him. But why do they have to go through me. I answer the phone when they call. Enough already.

Kel

------Email-------

Staci Parks looked like a young version of a shrewd politician. Although she sat in her bedroom surrounded by teddy bears, she could have been in a smoke-filled back room working on a deal. She was dressed in the latest, most expensive clothes. Her apparel was synchronized with her light red hair and scattered freckles making her seem older than she was. The new cell phone in her hand was not affordable for most adults, much less a 13-year-old seventh grader. Her young, determined, hazel eyes looked out at a world of potential opportunities. Growing up in affluent Normandy Park, she knew about what was in and what was 'so not cool'. After planning for some time, now it was time to act. She took one last spin around her well laid out scheme. *Maybe I should do more research before I call him,* she thought. *No, I think I'm ready. Oh yes, I think I'm.*

Staci was the new girl at school, but that did not stop her from becoming the central player in the seventh grade social scene. She had been watching Colt O'Brien since the beginning of the school year. After finding out all she could about him, she now had a plan. For her, only the most popular and exciting boy would do. She thought about how perfect it would be if they were together. *It has to be him. The rest are stupid and boring. And he lives in Normandy Park, like me. Just like Mom said, 'If you want something, you have to go after it'. Well, it's now or never.*

~~~

Colt sat on the plush couch in the living room of the O'Brien home. It was a spacious well furnished residence but not ostentatious. Although his family was well off, for Normandy Park, they lived rather simply. He half listened to his sister, Kelly, as she asked him about one of his least interesting subjects, girls. To him it seemed like his sister was wasting her breath as usual.

"Hey, I don't have time for girls. For some reason they like me, I guess," said Colt.

Kelly's short blond hair flipped up as she skipped over to her little brother. She shoved his shoulder and yelled in his ear.

"I'm sick of answering the phone and having some stupid, giggly girl on the other end or worse, more than one," she said.

Colt lightly pushed her away and smiled.

"What can I do? I don't tell them to call. I'm not into the girlfriend, boyfriend thing," said Colt.

"Well little bro, you better start thinking about it. This isn't going away. I think it would easier, for me, if you just had a girlfriend. Then I would only have to deal with one."

13

The shrill ringing of the phone interrupted their conversation. Kelly glared at Colt with a knowing look as she picked up the phone.

"Hello," said Kelly.

"Hi, is this Kelly?" said a syrupy sweet voice.

Kelly smiled a bit.

"Yes, this is Kelly. Who is this?"

"Hi Kelly. This is Staci Parks. We haven't met, but I think you're a great soccer player."

Colt saw a suspicious look on his sister's face. He always liked to see her get this way. He felt like he was seeing the real her.

"How old are you, Staci?" asked Kelly.

"Oh, I'm thirteen. Why do you ask?" came back a seemingly innocent reply.

Kelly's face became red as she looked to the ceiling in frustration.

"Do you want my little brother? Is that it?"

"Well, that is why I called. But, I hope we can get to know each other, too," answered Staci.

Kelly rolled her eyes and stuck a finger into her open mouth in disgust. She pushed the phone at Colt, who was looking on with curious eyes.

Kelly screamed at Colt, "This has to stop."

Colt could not help laughing at seeing his sister in such a state. *Ha, ha. Is she flipping out or what? I have to see who's on the phone.*

Still laughing, Colt grabbed the phone from his sister who stomped out of the room

"Hi Colt. This is Staci Parks. We have geography class together."

Colt racked his brain to remember who this was. *Oh, it's the new girl, the pretty one with the red hair.*

"Er, uh, hi Staci. What's up?"

"I was wondering if you would answer a question I have?"

"Um, sure. No problem."

Staci thought about her carefully planned blueprint for success. She hesitated while formulating the right words to achieve her desired outcome.

"You know, I love how you dress. All my girlfriends do, too. All the other boys are so boring, but you have a special style with clothes."

Colt was now relaxed and listening. He was proud of his special style.

"Yeah, I sorta like bright stuff."

"I made a bet with my girlfriends about why you dress like that. If you tell me, maybe I can win the bet."

"Sure, I can. One day I lost a baseball game. I was about ten, I think. My mom came in my room to cheer me up. She played a game where I put on the weirdest combination of clothes I could find. By the time we were done, I felt way better. So, I kept doing it, just not as weird. And, I always feel good when I wear bright clothes."

"Oh! Oh! I won my bet. This is great," Staci lied.

"So, you guessed right then?" said Colt.

"Yes, I guessed right. Maybe I can sorta tell what you're like. After all, I had the right answer."

Both of them took a breath and said nothing.

Staci thought, *now to seal the deal.*

"I was thinking, Colt... Maybe we could hang out together. You know, like go to the mall or something."

Colt now was wondering what to say. *No girl has asked me this before.*

15

"Er, uh, um, I've never done stuff like that," he said.

"Don't worry, Colt, I can set up everything. It will be fun, just the two of us. Okay?"

"Uh, sure. Okay," he said without knowing why.

End quick before he changes his mind, thought Staci.

"Great. I'll call you back later. Bye."

"Bye Staci."

Colt looked up from the couch and noticed that his sister had slipped back into the room and was sitting in a chair across from him. *Crap, was she there the whole time?*

Kelly smiled and asked, "Well, little bro, what happened?"

"I have a date, I guess," he said.

"How did that happen to a guy who is not into that girl stuff?" smiled Kelly.

"I have no idea," said Colt.

Chapter 4

------Email-------
From: Carbon, Bill[billg@hocs.biz]
To: Sweden, Gunnar[gunman@yahoo.com]
Subject: Are we ready yet

```
Hey Gunman
Bin studng all day til nowcan't close my eyes
without seeing test answers flyng by. bucks and
music keep me goin.
I guess I better hit the sack. Are we really
ready????????

later.....billgee
```

------Email-------

The October morning was bright and brisk. A black, compact, Nissan pickup truck was moving north along Perimeter Road, which bordered Boeing Field just south of the skyscrapers of Seattle, Washington. Dark, gray banks of clouds were rolling in from the Puget Sound to the west. The warm sun radiated into the cab, washing a middle-aged man and a young teenager in a golden glow. Both used sunglasses to filter the bright sun. The man, Matthew Carbon, wore a canvas baseball-style cap and gray t-shirt with faded jeans. His son, Billy, wore a long-sleeved black shirt with yellow vertical stripes and black slacks. In his hand was a tall Starbucks cup. He listened to music through small, lightweight headphones. The younger Carbon lifted his sunglasses to look at sheets of paper in his lap.

His bright blue eyes were tired, but focused. A manic energy poured from them, as if it would devour anything or anyone put in their path. The pale face revealed a lack of sleep, but those brilliant eyes were very awake.

Matthew tapped his son's arm and turned on the windshield wipers as the first light raindrops hit the Nissan's cracked windshield.

Billy pulled off his headphones, still staring at the notes. "Uh, yeah?"

"Do you have any more questions, Billy?" said Matthew.

"Do you think I'm ready? I feel like I've studied for a year."

"I know you're ready. Ron and I will give you and Gunnar some tips before you go in. You've done all the right things except for getting a good night's sleep."

"Yeah, I crammed. I really crammed," smiled Billy as he stretched his arms and yawned.

"If you don't already know the material, cramming doesn't help much. You would've been better off sleeping. The exam is two hours long. You need the energy," said Matthew.

"Don't worry. I have enough energy, Dad. I'm almost 15. No big deal."

"You're probably right, but old guys like me need our sleep or we crash and burn. I guess it's too late to worry about it now."

A steady rain fell as the pickup pulled into the parking lot of Wings Aloft on the east side of the Boeing Field tarmac. Small aircraft and another two-story building were next to the main building of the flight training school. The pair walked into the main area with its high ceiling and windows. There was a long check-in counter. Plush sofas and chairs littered the large waiting area. There was also a medium sized work table.

Ron and Gunnar Sweden waited for them, smiling with excitement. Ron wore his usual suit and tie. Gunnar, who was three inches shorter than his six-foot, two-inch father, wore a white t-shirt with the word "Doom" splashed across the front. Both father and son were thin with brown eyes. They were almost identical except for Gunnar's short black hair and his father's dark brown hair.

As the men and boys met, Gunnar said to Billy, "You need to sign in at the desk. Did you bring your birth certificate and social security card?"

"I have all that stuff. It'll be a lot easier when we have driver's licenses," said Billy.

Gunnar beamed with excitement. His brown eyes sparkled with anticipation.

"Man, this will be awesome. I think we can kick ass."

Billy also felt the excitement, but he managed to rein in the emotional team of horses pulling at him.

"Hey, it's our first time. Let's see what happens," he said.

Billy walked to the front desk with a steady determined stride. He pulled out the required identifications and laid the documents on the counter.

"I'm scheduled to take the Microsoft NT four workstation test." he said.

The short, blond, chubby girl behind the counter looked up with a friendly smile. She was in her mid-twenties, but seemed like a high school girl to Billy.

"Aren't you guys a little young for this exam? I've never seen this before. Usually, I see older guys who are out of school and working already."

The pale boy looked at the blond girl with a hint of pride through mature, steely eyes beneath a head of disheveled hair.

"I want to see if I can pass. Wouldn't that be great? Maybe it will help me get a fantastic job some day," answered Billy.

When she heard him speak, she felt embarrassed that she had doubted the student facing her. She could sense that this was not an average kid. She decided to treat this customer like an adult.

"I guess since you'll be testing at almost the same time, I can take you both up to show you the room and tell you the rules. When he goes in, you can come, too. I'll call you when it's time."

"Thank you," said Billy.

Billy walked back to the other three, who were smiling while they talked. He thought about the experience ahead. He felt exhilarated and afraid at the same time. The whole idea of passing a Microsoft Certification exam was exciting. *I still have to actually go into the room and do it. It will be just me and all those questions. I hope I studied enough. I guess I won't know until I do it.*

"Hey guys, we have about 30 minutes until Gunnar goes in. We have some things to discuss," said Matthew.

"Dad, the lady said I should go in with Gunnar to see how it's done," said Billy.

"That's fine. Now, listen to Ron and then we can discuss strategy," said Matthew.

Ron Sweden stood erect and beamed. His light brown eyes exuded optimism and confidence. He pointed to a large plush couch that was situated near floor-to-ceiling windows in a corner of the room.

"Gentlemen, please sit." he said.

After the boys were comfortable he gathered himself and spoke.

"Before you start, just know that we are extremely proud of you, no matter what happens. If either of you have problems with the exam today, we'll do whatever it takes to help you for the next time. You'll pass. It might not be today, but you'll pass. We all know that Microsoft makes this bad boy extremely difficult. This is for computing pros to show that they're qualified. There are questions that are difficult for Mr. Carbon and he's been doing this for years. This might be an historic day. No one this young has ever passed. Good luck to you both, even though we all know that you've made your own luck by working so hard. Mr. Carbon has a few words to say."

Both boys had become increasingly confident and energized while Ron Sweden talked. Now, they were smiling and sitting erect. Each young man had the look of a well-trained solder, ready for battle. Neither had any doubt about the outcome of their tests.

Matthew Carbon looked at the two and spoke.

"I have a few tips for you guys. The first test is always the hardest, because you've never been through it before. Any questions before I start?"

"What is the hardest part of taking one of these?" asked Gunnar.

"The questions are tricky. They go in one direction in the beginning and then change at the end. You need to double check to see that you actually understood the answer that they are looking for. I have some more things to tell you. First, answer every question. If you aren't sure, answer it anyway, mark it, and come back later. Read every question at least twice before answering. If you have a mind cramp, stop to refocus. Don't hurt yourself by getting too frustrated over one question. You guys know the material. If you stay calm, you'll get enough right. And, one last thing, this is pass or fail. In the end, the score doesn't matter."

The blond young woman came over and asked the boys to follow her. They walked behind her out the door toward the field. The fathers looked through the windows as the three walked up the stairs of a small two-story, blue building. After about five minutes, Billy and the girl came back. Billy immediately started to read through a large hardcover book and a pile of notes.

Matthew Carbon looked at Ron Sweden. The confidence he demonstrated minutes before had disappeared. His shoulders were slumped and he was staring at the blue building. Matthew could see that he was tense. The two men walked away from Billy. Ron looked seriously at Matthew and spoke.

"I've been over the material. I'm not a computer expert, but it looks extremely difficult. Are these kids prepared for this? I would hate to see them fail after all of that hard work."

Matthew Carbon looked up to the much taller man and smiled.

"This is their first exam. I made sure that they studied more than necessary. They know it inside and out. We only have the emotional factor. That's the unknown. We have no way of knowing how much pressure they'll put on themselves? I think they're too young to feel it. I'm very optimistic. We'll know soon."

Ron looked drained and forsaken in spite of the other man's words.

"I wish I was as confident as you are."

This guy can sure turn it on when he wants, but I guess he's human like the rest of us. I never thought he doubted anything. Man, those kids thought they could walk on water after he got through with them, thought Matthew.

Billy was now coming over. It was time for him to go in. He shook hands with both parents and smiled. He seemed almost frisky.

"I'm as ready as I'll ever be. I've decided this is going to be fun, no matter what."

After watching Billy walk up the stairs, the men waited. Neither man sat as the minutes oozed by like thick, sticky syrup. They walked and talked, while occasionally looking out the tall windows, through the rain, at the closed door at the top of the stairs. Although the exam was scheduled for two hours, both fathers started staring directly at the door after an hour and a half. Finally, the door opened and Gunnar stepped onto the platform. He looked neither happy nor sad, but a bit distracted. The men gestured as if to ask, "What happened? Did you pass?" Ron Sweden was especially expressive and intense. Gunnar slowly looked over and acted as if he had not seen anyone. It seemed like time stopped for the fathers. Then Gunnar smiled and thrust his arm out with a thumb shooting toward the dark sky. Both men clapped and Ron Sweden jumped a little. They walked briskly to the door as the tall boy leapt down the stairs in glee.

"What was it like?" beamed Ron Sweden to his son.

"I got 820. It was okay after I stopped worrying. It took me until Billy showed up to calm down."

"How hard was it?

"We really do know this stuff. Mr. Carbon was right. We just needed to stay cool. Billy was going fast. I think he'll be out soon. Oh, and I found a question that was wrong. I gave the answer they wanted though."

As Gunnar went to the front desk to get the official read-out of his exam score, the fathers walked out the door and waited near the bottom of the steps. There was a light mist gently blowing onto them. Gunnar was walking up to them when the door at the top of the stairs opened. Billy walked out grinning and raised both arms into the air. The two fathers and Gunnar clapped and cheered.

Billy yelled, "I did it! I got an 800! Wow, is this great!"

After the boys had calmed down a little, the still radiant Ron Sweden pulled two baseball-style caps out of a bag and handed one to each boy.

He said, "You're both Microsoft Certified Professionals now. That's what it says on these hats. This is good; this is very good."

Chapter 5

------Email-------
From: O'Brien, Colt[ColtOB@yahoo.com]
To: Jones, Bobby[Bobbyj@yahoo.com]
Subject: What the hell?
Sent: 10/15/1999

What the hell is goin on Bobster? I saw some computer thing going on in the tech lab. Creepy snotnosed kids barely out of 6th grade were acting computer smart. That's our room. I don't trust them.........

------Email-------

Colt O'Brien flashed down the main hall of Highline High School. The five foot, four-inch senior was dressed to garner attention. He strutted like he owned the town of Burien and the State of Washington. His jet-black hair, dark blue eyes and unique style of dress made him stand out. He wore purple tennis shoes, gray T-shirt, red shorts with a day-glo orange backpack that bounced up and down his back. Crowds of students were strolling between classes and talking in small groups. Although this was nothing new, they looked up to see what color combinations were on display today. Colt's rapid strides and decisive, churning arm movements made the other students seem stationary. Suddenly, a piercing, monotonous sound pealed through the air, causing Colt to stop. Students moved away from him as he grabbed something from his belt. He held the small, black, rectangular noise-maker between his thumb and forefinger. He looked around and waved it at the onlookers.

"Haven't you heard a pager before? It's not a fire alarm. Chill out. I have another computer to fix, that's all."

A high-pitched male voice from the crowd whined, "Can't you make that thing stop beeping. Isn't there a silent mode or something?"

"Whatever," said Colt with a shrug. "Later dude, later."

He looked at the message on the pager which read, "911 – Mr. Towne's computer is down - Please come to office."

Colt grinned and thought about how much he liked his life. *I love being a senior; only a few easy classes to sit through. I get to save the principal of the school from his computer and from himself.* He beamed with pride in knowing that he was the hero, the answer man, the tech guy that always saved the day. Bringing computers back to life gave him a deep, lasting satisfaction. *To most of them, computers are magic. Good for me. Nobody is as good at this stuff as I am.* He was already beginning to sparkle as he pranced decisively toward the office and another opportunity to demonstrate his skills.

Colt slowed down as he approached Mr. Towne's office. A woman in her forties with dark red hair and a friendly smile sat behind a desk. Her bright blue eyes twinkled as Colt walked in.

"That was fast. You were either close or you ran all the way," she said.

"Hi Janet. I was close, but you know I'd hustle over here anyway. So what happened this time?" said Colt.

"Mr. Towne said the screen went blank and never came back. I just checked and it's still that way. He's in a meeting. Go on in. By the way, your shoes are my color. How did you know?"

Colt liked that Janet was being playful. He tried to put those who he helped at ease. The young man grinned.

"I always try to give great service to my customers. And a little color can brighten someone's day."

"Well, it brightened mine," said Janet with a smile.

Colt strolled into the office while removing his backpack, which he laid on the floor in front of an upright, gray, rectangular computer. He paused to look at the bulky video monitor that was sitting on the large desk above. The screen was blank. He then surveyed the computer itself and pushed a button. The plain gray box emitted a soft whirring sound for a few seconds and was silent. After about five seconds he pushed the button again. Three small lights blinked and the whirring sound started again. The computer monitor flashed on and off numerous times before Colt pushed the power button again to turn the machine off. With sure hands, he removed cables from the rear of the personal computer and laid it on its side. After unscrewing the side panel, he located and yanked out a plastic electronic card that was about four inches long by three inches wide. He put the card into his backpack and walked out of the room to Janet's desk.

"It's the video card. I'll grab one and be back in a bit," said Colt.

"How bad is it? I'm not even going to ask what a video card is. I hate those things," said Janet.

"No big deal. It doesn't look that bad. I hate those things myself sometimes," he said with eyes looking toward the ceiling.

Colt exited the office and strolled down the hall, which was now empty. At the end, he walked down a flight of stairs to the basement floor. He opened the door to the second room on the left and walked in under a sign that read TECH LAB. Then he encountered the unexpected.

A loud voice echoed through the room, which startled Colt. He looked up to see four people. One person was in front of a

27

white board that displayed black, scribbled words. *That guy looks like a teacher. But why is he here shouting so loud?* Three others sat at a table that was about six feet long, listening. *Who the hell are these guys? Don't they know this is our tech room?* He stiffened and looked at the interlopers with an untrusting stare. It took all of the self-control he could muster to avoid questioning the invaders. He nodded to the group as he shuffled past them toward another room in the back. They acknowledged by nodding back and returned to what they had been doing.

Colt pretended to be busy as he watched what appeared to be an informal computer class. He noticed the words on the white board first: TCP/IP, Sub-netting, DHCP, Host Header, and others. The only acronym that he recognized was TCP/IP, which he knew had something to do with the internet. The rest of the words were foreign to him. The medium-sized man with the booming voice wore a gray T-shirt, faded jeans and a tan baseball cap that had the word "Microsoft" sewn onto the front. He had mixed blue-green eyes, was a bit stocky, and spoke casually, but with a deep confident voice. One of the three listeners was also an adult. He was tall and slender with intelligent brown eyes. He listened, but had a confused look which Colt could relate to. His tailored suit fit him perfectly and he was obviously comfortable wearing it. Colt guessed his age at around forty-five. Next to him sat two young boys that he did not recognize. *Crap! They have to be freshmen. These guys look way too relaxed. If I don't know this stuff, then there's no way they do. They have to be punks faking it. This feels like total crap.*

Colt became more agitated and was about to become angry. His mind was no longer working in a logical fashion and he knew it. *I better wait before I talk to these guys. They're already pissing me off.*

His attention now turned to an overhead cabinet, which he unlocked and opened. An assortment of computer components and devices including mice and keyboards, were piled in a disorganized heap. Colt grabbed a computer card that was the same size as the one he removed from Mr. Towne's PC and shoved it into his backpack. As he did so, he removed the defective card from his backpack and dropped it in a three-by-three-foot clear plastic bin that had "BAD PARTS" scrawled on the side in black magic marker. He said nothing as he scurried past the four intruders and out the door.

Janet glanced up from her desk as a Colt entered the office. He winked as he passed her, but was forced to stop when he strode through the office doorway, causing his backpack to bounce up his back. Someone occupied the chair in front of the dead computer and desk. If his teenage reflexes had not been so acute, he would've plowed into Mr. Towne.

Mr. Towne, the principal of Highline High, looked at Colt and said "Good to see you, Colt. You never know when these things are going to break, I guess."

His kind smile reflected a strong affection for the young man. For many years he had felt that there was a connection between them. He was only about two inches taller than Colt and had a keen understanding of what it was like to be the shortest guy in the room. He also liked Colt's work ethic and confidence as well as his passion. He was well aware of the young man's temper tantrums, but tended to overlook them when possible.

This kid sure has talent when it comes to computers, thought Mr. Towne.

"Hello Mr. Towne. If you let me get in there, I can get you working again. It's just a video card."

"Thanks. I needed to hear that. I've got loads of email to read, even if most of it is a waste of time." answered the kind man with a smile.

Mr. Towne stood up and moved away from the desk as Colt pulled out the video card from his backpack. He inserted the card into a slot inside the personal computer, turned it upright, reconnected the cables, and flipped on the power switch. The entire procedure took less than five minutes. The monitor on the desk flashed and then went black with white lines of text moving up the screen. After a minute the familiar icons and menus of Microsoft Windows displayed on the screen.

An amazed Mr. Towne said, "Thanks Colt. You did it again."

"Glad I could help. Uh, er, I was wondering about something."

"What would that be?" asked Mr. Towne.

"I saw some people in the Tech Lab. It was like a class or something. What's up with that?" asked Colt.

The energetic principal smiled with pride.

"We're starting a new computer class. It's a new Microsoft certification. Mr. Sweden and Mr. Carbon started the program with their sons. We're now making it a part of our curriculum."

No goddam way. That's my territory. Screw these guys, thought Colt.

"Why are they using the Tech Room?" blurted out Colt with a bit more force than was necessary.

"They needed a temporary place. It won't be for long, and I approved it. Tell the other tech guys."

"What's a certification? I never heard of it?"

"It shows that you are qualified on certain computer skills. I'll tell Mr. Sweden that you have an interest in the program. He can give you the details."

"No need to do that. I was just wondering. I'll tell the Tech Squad guys that it's okay for those guys to use the lab. Uh, I better get going."

Colt screwed the computer back together and headed for the door.

"You should check into this new class, Colt. I think it'll be a good opportunity for you," said Mr. Towne.

But, Colt O'Brien was already gone.

Chapter 6

```
------Email-------
From: Parks, Staci[sparks@aol.com]
To: O'Brien, Kelly[Kellyobrien@UW.org]
Subject: sad about colt
---------------------------------------------------------------------
```

hi kel
why can't colt see that im as important as his stupid computers/
i miss him sooooo much/ Im sad, sad, sad XXXXXX/
can i call and cry on your shoulder

staci


```
------Email-------
```


Colt sat in the back seat of the black Lexus in the driveway of his home in Normandy Park, Washington. Cold rain pelted the car's roof. His mother, Leona, sat in the passenger seat with his father behind the wheel. Colt's parents were respected and popular. Robert was a successful, insurance executive and Leona a stay-at-home mom who volunteered for charity work. Both were an integral part of the Normandy Park social scene. Robert O'Brien's distinguished, commanding appearance was somehow in sync with the petite, attractive Leona, in spite of their size difference.

"Robert, let's get going. I don't want to miss anything," said Leona.

"Don't worry sweetheart, I'll get us there on time," answered Colt's father in a confident tone.

Colt sat in the back seat in deep thought. His mind jumped from one topic to another: the new computer class, his ex-girlfriend Staci, Mr. Towne… *I can't keep track of all of this stuff. Man, mental overload. Slow down, dude, or you'll never stop your mind from spinning in circles.* One thing that Colt was wrestling with was his latest unsolvable computer problem. It was a catastrophic event that happened often called "The Blue Screen of Death". The symptom of the problem was that the video screen turned blue and the computer stopped working or "hung". When this happened, Colt was always able to restore a machine to usability, but he had not been able to determine a root cause. *Crap, I need to know why that happens. I can't give up on this. Maybe I can find some info on the internet.*

As the Lexus entered the on-ramp to Interstate 5, heading north, Colt sensed a change in the mood. His inner vision displayed a movie-like scene where soft tentacles slithered over the front seat at him. They probed, trying to feel him out. He wanted to think that his mind was making things up, but he had a strong feeling it was his usual inner radar telling him something was coming. *What now? And I thought I would be left alone back here.*

Then, he thought to himself, *Oh no, not the lecture. I really don't need the lecture right now.*

The lecture consisted of Robert telling Colt about distinguishing himself in life and making his parents proud, like his sister Kelly. She was an honor student at The University of Washington and also played on the women's soccer team. He'd had enough comparisons to his sister to last a lifetime. Since the family's destination was one of Kelly's games at the University of Washington campus, he expected the worst.

"Colt, how are you doing back there?" asked Robert.

Colt braced himself and tried to figure out how to avoid dealing with what was coming.

"Okay Dad. I hope Kelly wins today."

"Your mother and I have been wondering about your future. We thought this would be a good time to discuss some things."

"Yes honey, we're wondering about what you've done as far as college? You know how important that is," said Leona.

In spite of his mother's loving, singsong voice, which usually soothed the teenager, he now looked at the windows and doors like a caged animal.

"Can't this wait? I have other stuff on my mind right now."

The space in the car became imbued with tension as Robert inhaled and formed his thoughts.

"Listen to me. You're a part of a family that achieves great things. Your sister has led the way. Now it's your turn," said Robert.

Crap, the old man is into it. My sister has what? Screw this. Here we go again.

"Robert, don't browbeat him. He tries," said Leona.

"I've had enough of his wasting time on computers. It's time for him to grow up. The world has enough losers," said Robert.

"What's wrong with working on computers? Computers will change the world," yelled Colt.

"Just stop now, both of you. This is supposed to be a fun family outing," cried Leona.

"This isn't over, Colt. I won't let you throw your life away surfing the web or whatever you do. Life is not a computer game," said Robert.

Colt knew better than to try to get in the last word with his father. After years of trying, he'd learned that his father would not allow it. He stared out of his window at the gray sky. These trips to his sister's games were the only family activity that Colt still enjoyed. *What a way to mess up a good thing. I hope this BS stops now*. Robert, who was now incensed, gripped the wheel and glared straight ahead at the highway. Not a word was spoken for the remainder of the ride.

In the parking lot of the soccer field on the university campus, Robert opened the trunk of the Lexus and passed out blankets and assorted pieces of clothing. It was still raining lightly and they came prepared for anything. Colt scanned the field and the stately, orange brick buildings on the hill above. His smile reflected the feelings of hope and achievement that he always sensed on this campus. Although he didn't like being compared to Kelly, he had great affection for her and enjoyed her success.

In spite of the words in the car, the mood of family changed as they approached the soccer field. All three were united in their desire to see Kelly, and her team, succeed. Colt soon forgot about the ride while cheering for his sister. Robert and Leona also loved competition and became caught up in the excitement of the game. The game was especially enjoyable for the entire family because of Kelly's play and the outcome. Kelly scored one of the two goals in the win. After the game, Leona waved as her daughter walked gracefully toward the sideline. She was radiant, even though most of her purple uniform was soaking wet and muddy. Her trim, athletic, five-foot, seven-inch frame, short blond hair, and sparkling light blue eyes set her apart. Colt could see why she was receiving offers to model.

"Hi, everyone. We kicked butt. Those California girls hate the rain," said Kelly with a grin.

"Great game, sweetheart. Good goals," said Robert.

"Oh Kelly, I was so excited. We're so proud of you," said Leona.

"I need to get back to the locker room, but I want to talk to little brother for a minute. Can I call you guys later?" asked Kelly.

"Sure sweetheart. We'll talk later," said Robert as he and Leona headed back to the car.

"Hi Sis, awesome game," said Colt.

"How is it goin'? Still fixin' those broken computers?"

"Yeah. You know I love the techy stuff."

"I'm getting an earful from Mom and Dad about you. And Staci called me. She sure works the angles."

Colt flinched a little. He was very happy that he and Staci weren't together. And, he wanted it to stay that way.

"Here it comes. So, do you have a Colt list or something? What did they say?"

Sensing Colt's displeasure, Kelly put her arm around her little brother kissing him lightly on the cheek.

"Hey little Bro, I'm just the messenger. Anyway, Staci misses you and wants to get back together. She thinks computers are the problem. I think Mom and Dad will have the big talk with you soon, the future and all that," said Kelly.

"Mom and Dad started pounding on me on the ride here, so I know what they want. But with Staci, I don't know and I don't care. Chicks, what a pain. Except you, of course. We were together for years and now it's like she wants to control everything."

"I hate to tell you this, but she was always that way."

"Yeah, but I could always dodge her when I wanted to before. I just got fed up. I'm done with her," said Colt.

"I think if you didn't spend so much time on computers it would be a lot better. You gotta have other stuff goin' on, too. Time for me to go. Love ya."

The siblings hugged.

"Bye Sis. I love you, too."

Kelly loped across the field and was soon gone.

Colt walked back to the car thinking about the growing list of things to deal with. *No way I'm going back with Staci. I'm sick of her trying to control everything I do. I need to forget all this crap. It's driving me nuts.*

Colt smiled as an inner light bulb blinked on. *I know just the thing to loosen me up. Time to forget about this crap.*

Chapter 7

------Email-------
From: O'Brien, Colt[ColtOB@yahoo.com]
To: Jones, Bobby[bobbyj@yahoo.com]
Subject: Let's meet

Boberto
Let's meet at the club for rball. How about 9am sat. I need to get sane. We can talk about the little nerds and the computer stuff too.

------Email-------

The two friends, covered in sweat, played with abandon. Colt, the shorter of the two, moved with grace, quickness and tenacity. Bobby, a head taller, but not as quick, still managed to keep up. He was helped by his strength, experience and that the enclosure was small allowing him to reach with his long arms and legs. The small, blue, rubber ball flashed around the racquetball enclosure, causing reverberating echoes. Colt yammered constantly adding to the bouncing sounds. He teased, cajoled and screamed at his friend Bobby, who was concentrating like his life depended on every shot. The two friends complemented each other. Colt was a leader with confidence and a healthy competitive nature. Bobby was steady and even tempered. He lived his life according to the rules. No rocking any boats for young Mr. Jones. Colt took risks while his friend played it as safe as possible.

Bobby's mother once said of her only child, "Does my little boy ever even think about being a little naughty? It's like he was born a grown up."

"He'll make us look like perfect parents, even if he does bore us to death," her husband replied.

Bobby shuffled toward the right wall and waited for the blue blur to come to him. He squatted and hit the ball just above the floor. His racquet struck the ball on the sweet spot. It moved so fast that Colt did not see it until it was rolling flat on the floor, the result of a perfect, un-defensible kill shot.

"That's game," said Bobby.

"Dude, dude, no way! You aren't good enough to beat me. Are you sure you got the score right?" yelled Colt with his hands thrust out.

"Don't get into your act, man. You know I won. It's all tied up. Are you ready to stop or what?" Bobby replied.

"Quit? I don't think so, Bobbysoxer. I'll beat you, even if you do get creative with the score."

Colt had fire in his eyes, but smiled as he turned away.

Bobby's body tensed and his face reddened. "Creative? That's bull! You keep score then! You keep score! Let's see what you've got, Colt. I'm ready. Bring it on!" he yelled.

Colt won the final game as he had expected. He poked a weak spot in his friend's defenses and gained an edge. Nothing could make Colt happier.

Oh dude. You fell for it. Man, you're soooooo easy.

"Dude, dude. You lost your focus. How could that happen?" laughed Colt.

Bobby looked at his friend with a hint of anger and respect.

"You got me again. If you didn't play those mind games, you'd never win."

39

The young men had danced this dance for many years. The relationship worked because each was comfortable with his own role. There was a special blend of character traits between them that manifested as true friendship.

"Bobinator, let's get latte'd up and you can tell me about this new computer thing," said Colt.

"After getting me so mad that I lost, you can buy," said Bobby. He knew Colt was attempting to smooth out the emotional terrain after baiting him, yet again. The sting was almost gone, but he didn't think that Colt needed to know that.

~~~

The Burien Starbucks near the Athletic Club had opened doors for business a few months earlier. People were lined up in anticipation, waiting to order lattes, cappuccinos and other assorted coffee beverages. The little café had become a social center of this little town near Sea-Tac Airport, as had other stores in other towns across the Northwest. A sense of cool permeated the air along with the aroma of roasted coffee and assorted pastries.

The friends ordered and after waiting for about ten minutes, grabbed their sugar-laced coffee drinks and found a place to sit. Colt spoke.

"I'm really sick of getting pushed around. My parents think I'm slacking on the school stuff. My dad said computer guys are losers."

Colt felt a large release of frustration after expressing his feelings. Bobby took a sip of his steaming drink and looked at Colt like a school administrator or parent.

"Hey, man. You need to get it together. I'm enrolled at Western for next year. Why not go there with me?"

"I'm into computers, not more school. You know I'm sick of boring stuff. I want to do computer work and make money," said Colt.

"I want to make money too and have stability. My parents say no degree, no money. At least not that much money." said Bobby. Colt realized he would get no support from his friend and decided to change the subject.

"I see this is going nowhere. You sound like my mom and dad. Let's talk about something else."

"Hey man, it's just common sense. I'm going to college first. What about the Staci thing? Is that really over after being together so long?" asked Bobby.

"It's done. She wants to control me all the time. And she's getting on my nerves. It took a while, but I've had enough."

"Man, you were together a long time."

"I think she had our lives planned out for the next twenty years. Only problem is she forgot to ask me," said Colt.

After impatiently waiting for the topic of conversation to move in the direction he wanted, Colt took charge.

"So, tell me about this new computer class. Where did it come from?"

"I talked to Jimmy Gruber. He tried it out. He said you study like a dog and then take tests. It's some Microsoft thing."

"If he can do it, then it has to be easy. I love everything about Microsoft, but I've never heard of this," said Colt.

"Jimmy said it was harder than hell. He tried one practice test after wading through pages of stuff and totally bombed. He ran for cover, man. No way I'm doing it."

"What about those punk kids I saw in the Tech Lab? I bet it's like when the dad is a coach of the little league team and his kid gets to pitch. " asked Colt.

41

"It was started by two freshman kids and their dads. It must have been them. I guess one of the dads is into computers. Jim said he taught the classes," said Bobby.

"So, you're telling me that those punk kids have passed some of the tests? How could they if they're so hard?"

"Uh, I think they have. Jim said that Mr. Towne thinks this will put Highline High on the map. He calls it High Tech Learning or something. They're getting some publicity already and a few kids are trying it. They hold classes wherever they can and there's a lot of self-study."

"What are the tests for? Why are they so hard?"

"I think it's for something called NT and network stuff. I don't know much about that, just Windows on PCs," said Bobby.

"Hey Bobster, we know computers. It can't be that hard. I haven't done anything with that either, but I can learn it. You'll be asking me for answers in no time. I'm still the number one computer guy."

Bobby leaned forward and looked directly at Colt with raised eyebrows.

"I know you were the best, but it looks to me like the competition has arrived."

Bobby smiled inwardly as he saw Colt's eyes change into piercing laser beams. He knew that Colt was frustrated that his world view was being modified by reality.

"You have to know this is total crap. I bet the dads are taking the tests. How can some freshmen know more than us? You watch. This'll turn into nothing. Those little nerd wannabes will fade away."

"Sure, whatever. A lot of people think these kids are the real deal. Why don't you take a test and we'll see what happens?"

"Dude, I'm on it. They won't know what hit them."

But, Colt was feeling a little queasy. His inner radar sensed alien objects approaching and sirens were clanging in his head. He had no answers to the numerous questions flashing across his inner landscape. *Why is Mr. Towne into this? How can those kids be that smart? Why is it such a big deal?*

But, when he walked out of Starbucks into a soft, misty, rain, a logical inner voice told him that he was wrong about the new kids on the block and their certification program. He sensed that it was time to prepare for a big, big change.

Chapter 8

------Email-------
From: Sweden, Gunnar[gunman@yahoo.com]
To: Carbon, Billy[billg@hocs.biz]
Subject: Whats goin on
----

billg

studying for network essentials test. It's all starting to look the same. i even have dreams where I see IP adresses. i must be getting smart

gunman

------Email-------

Two young boys sat at side-by-side computers with oversized video monitors. In the lower right corner of their respective screens, gaming nicknames of BillG and Gunman were displayed. With little effort, they typed, pounded and caressed the keyboards at the end of their fingertips. They both viewed different sections of the inside of a dark castle with corridors, doors, moats and multi-colored walls. Moving through the first-person-shooter game, they fired weapons at assorted, animated foes. Shotguns, grenades and machine guns were used as needed and changed often. Sounds rumbled through the bedroom as pixilated enemies were slain, only to have resurrected versions replace them.

Gunnar Sweden, Gunman and Billy Carbon, BillG were in Gunnar's upstairs bedroom in the Sweden home. Although the room was spacious, it was filled with computer equipment and stacks of books. At first glance it was difficult to know that it was really a bedroom.

Gunnar, the tall dark-haired boy, yelled, "Get him! Get him! No, no back, too many of them. Get out. Ahhhh!"

The smaller, brown-haired boy, Billy, said, "This is bad; dead again. Crap!"

"It's better with the two computers directly connected, way better," said Gunnar.

"I like team play. One on one gets boring. There's a lot more strategy this way," said Billy.

The boys were avid, experienced computer game players. Like many of their friends, they began playing computer games early. Now, at age fourteen, both were skilled players and also knew how to install, configure and troubleshoot game software as well as troubleshoot and fix computers. The problems and idiosyncrasies that challenged even seasoned computer technicians were simple to them.

Gunnar was now rapidly opening and closing different windows, using the computer's mouse and keyboard. He moved through different web sites on the internet and then opened a small black window and started typing text at a frantic pace. His hands and fingers flashed in a precise rhythm as the computer responded to his commands. Occasionally, he pounded the Enter key, causing the keyboard to bounce slightly. He manipulated the computer like a smooth, rapid violinist.

Billy interrupted.

"GunMan, let's get back on task. We need to work on our presentation."

After being ignored for a few minutes, Billy grabbed the other boy's shoulder and said into his ear, "Hey!"

Gunnar was awakened from his focused trance.

"Oh, uh yeah, we need to do that other thing, don't we?"

The two young boys looked on as the first page of a PowerPoint presentation displayed on the computer screen. The title read "Windows NT Memory Model". They dove into their next project.

~~~

Matthew Carbon was talking naturally, but his voice boomed through the large living room on the main floor of the Sweden home. While their sons worked upstairs, the fathers discussed strategies and approaches for the new certification program. The sun shone through the large picture window which looked onto the Puget Sound below. Ron Sweden was trying to understand what Matthew was saying, but cringed from the booming voice of his partner.

Ron moved closer to Matthew and quietly said, "Would you please lower your voice."

"Oh, I'm sorry. I get loud when I'm really focusing on something. Please let me know whenever that happens."

He concentrated and with a lowered voice spoke again.

"In the computer business, everyone works together. There are too many things to know and one push of a key can make bad things happen. Teamwork is the best approach."

"I'm not used to that. In my job I do everything myself. I'm rewarded for being independent and spontaneous. This idea of working together, as a team, is a new concept for Gunnar and me." said Ron.

"This program is an opportunity for kids to help each other achieve something by working together. But, when it's time for an exam they'll do it individually," said Matthew.

"You're the computer expert. If it's done that way in business then we should follow. So, how does it work?"

"Everybody is part of the team; the kids, the parents and the school. The front-runners like Gunnar and Billy will help teach the other kids. Also, students can work in groups if they're studying the same material." answered Matthew.

Ron grinned and nodded in understanding.

"I'll call the boys down and we can talk about their future."

Ron spoke with seriousness when he addressed the boys.

"Mr. Carbon and I have been discussing goals and ways to achieve those goals. He tells me that it's all done as a team. Mr. Carbon has a few things he wants to tell you."

"Already our little program is getting noticed. You guys are the first to pass any of the exams and are the leaders. I expect you'll be the center of attention, especially since you're so young. Enjoy your success, but stay humble. Always set a good example and do your best. Some people will want you to fail. Prove them wrong every time and do it with class. We're proud of both of you. We know you can meet the challenge."

Then Ron stepped in and addressed the young teenagers.

"Mr. Towne wants Highline High to be a computing leader in education. You guys have started something big. As part of the High Tech Learning Center we'll have what we need to make big things happen. Our books and other materials will come from the school."

"So Dad, what do we do when the older kids start giving us a hard time? Some guys on the Tech Squad already think we're trying to take over," asked Billy.

"If you can help them with something, do it. Ignore them if they give you lip. If they start to push you around, let one of us know. Okay?" said Matthew.

"Did you see Colt O'Brien give us the dirty eye in the Tech Lab? There is no way that he likes this," Gunnar added.

"Yeah, Flash doesn't like anybody to know more than him," said Billy.

"Who is flash?" asked Ron.

"That's our nickname for Colt O'Brien. It's because of his clothes," said Gunnar.

"I think we should recruit Mr. O'Brien. If he's good at fixing computers, then he might want to prove it. Let's call him by his real name though. He might think that the little freshmen are making fun of him." said Ron.

"Okay, Dad," said Gunnar. "Uh Dad, what is the High Tech Learning Center?"

"It's a program that supplies funding for different computer-related classes in member schools. Mr. Towne was able to get Highline into it and he thinks that we have the best class.

Matthew said, "You guys do the work and help the other kids. We can handle the other stuff."

"Okay, Dad," said Billy. "We only want to pass the tests and get certified."

Ron Sweden's eyes sparkled at the boys, highlighting a huge grin.

"This will be fantastic. All of your hard work will pay off, and you'll have a great time."

Gunman and BillG smiled. They didn't know what to expect, but knew it would be great. Ron Sweden's positive outlook and enthusiasm radiated into each of their young minds, promising success.

Chapter 9

------Email-------
From: O'Brien, Colt[ColtOB@yahoo.com]
To: Jones, Bobby[bobbyj@yahoo.com]
Subject: Getting pounded
----

my dad is totally pissed. this college thing has him ready to duke it out. Geez....

colt

------Email-------

Through a haze of disorientation Colt sensed that he was in the middle of a gathering. He couldn't see or hear anyone, but he knew they were there, bumping up against him. His eyes and ears were not functioning, but another psychic sense was feeling muted magnetic currents bouncing around him. *I wonder why things are like this. Where the hell am I? It's like they're all around me but hiding.* Colt gathered his thoughts and concentrated, but it was futile.

Finally, as he relaxed, giving up on the idea of seeing anything, a blob of unfocused colors began to take form. The less he tried to make it into something, the clearer it became. Just before the transformation was complete, he recognized that it was a familiar face. It was Staci. Oh*, no. I really don't want to see her right now. Why is it her?*

Staci's face was animated and serious. Her large hazel eyes looked right into his soul, while her lips pecked like a starving bird. *She looks different, sorta pretty. But it's still her.* He recognized a

49

familiar pattern and could guess what she was saying, but could not hear a word. *At least I can't hear her.* Colt was through with Staci talking about never spending time together, his obsession with computers, and how he didn't love her. *I've had enough of this. Time to tell her to get out of my life.* He opened his mouth to yell, but Staci flung both of her arms out and pushed him. He was stunned at the force. *Whoa, where did that come from? She has arms, too?* Colt's ex-girlfriend disappeared as he spun away and started falling. Down, down into nothingness he fell, twirling, flailing and screaming in silence. Then, it came to him. *Oh, I know this place. Now I remember that I've been here before. I'm in a dream.*

"Wake up, Colt, wake up." came a faraway voice.

Colt was shocked out of his dream state into reality. He could hear a light but firm tapping on his bedroom door and someone calling. Still feeling the effects of his dream, he tried to adjust to the real world. The first thing he noticed was that rain was boisterously pelting his bedroom window. It made him think of Staci's mouth moving. *At least I don't have to deal with Staci the bird girl anymore.*

"Colt, are you there? It's nine o'clock. I need you to get up," said his mother.

He sat up yawning, but made no effort to move off the bed.

"Hey, isn't it Saturday? Where's the fire?"

"I need to talk to you, sweetie, and it's important," she said.

"Give me some time to wake up and shower."

"Let's talk now. Put on some pajamas or something. The coffee and scones are ready."

Colt smiled at hearing the sweet sing-song voice of Leona. It was like delicate music hitting his emotional center.

Scones? Coffee? I'm up for that. Heck, I'm awake now anyway.

After throwing on some clothes, Colt opened his bedroom door. *Yeeow! What the hell!* A large hand grabbed him by the upper arm and yanked him into the hall. He looked up at his father, who appeared ready to squeeze him into a ball like play dough. *So, this wake-up call isn't so sweet after all. Crap, he trapped me when my special mind powers were weak with dreams. Man, if he's grabbing me like this, it can't be good.*

"Robert, you didn't have to do that. He was coming out. He isn't a common criminal," said Leona.

Colt's father, whose teeth were clenched, kept towing the much smaller Colt behind him. As he manhandled Colt down the hall, he would pull him up, causing his feet to leave the floor.

"I didn't want him to squirm out of this. He's like a trout that always slips out of our hands. It's time to have a real talk with our slippery fish." answered Robert.

"At least give me a cup of coffee so I can wake up," whined Colt.

His arm was starting to hurt from being pulled. *What did I do?*

Leona looked at Colt with pronounced worry wrinkles. She hit her husband on the chest to make him release Colt.

"Oh Colt honey, the coffee is in the den," she said.

Colt sat at the mahogany table that was the centerpiece of his father's den. A stack of fresh scones and a carafe of coffee rested on the table. Colt breathed in the aromas and tried to pull himself together. He slowly poured coffee into his cup while grabbing a scone. *This is like going to jail in your own house. At least they're feeding me.* Both he and his mother avoided this room. This was his father's center of power. He seemed to be at his most overbearing when sitting at his desk, in this room.

His parents sat on one side of the table with Colt on the other. He knew this was a special situation, but not what it was about. He said nothing while sipping the strong coffee and nibbling on a soft, fluffy scone. *I have to use my head and keep my mouth shut or I won't get out of here alive.* Colt attempted to look

51

innocent of whatever he might be accused of but I still wasn't awake enough to do an adequate acting job.

Robert stared at Colt with cold gray eyes.

"You lis..." he started to say.

Leona, who was half his size, started pounding his arm with her tiny hands and shaking her head from side to side.

"Don't you say a word! You said I could talk first!" she cried.

Robert, with a sheepish smile, looked at his red-faced wife.

"Okay honey, okay. Stop hitting me. I'll keep my word."

"Honey, Mr. Towne asked us to come in for a talk. He has a very high opinion of you," said Leona.

Hey, maybe I can relax. I know Mr. Towne is on my side.

"Good deal. I help him with his computer problems," said Colt.

"But honey, he said he's concerned about your future education. He asked us if you've applied to any colleges. We've talked about this so many times. We thought you were handling it."

"Yeah squirt. What's up with that? Have you done anything?" snarled his dad.

"Hey. No big deal. I've decided that school can wait a little while. I want to fix computers. I'm already making money doing it."

Leona's entire body sank and she frowned. Robert started to look like he would erupt. His fists were clenched and his face was beet red.

Oops, I guess that didn't go over too well.

"Don't even think about not going to college, Colt. I'll strangle you with my bare hands," yelled Robert.

"Uh, Bill Gates is a big wheel and he never did much college. He's the best computer guy around; rich, too." answered Colt.

"Computing is not a career for someone in our family. You need to start thinking about being a leader and being responsible."

Leona was visibly distraught. She frowned with her hands held to her heart.

"Colt, don't do this. Look at how well your sister is doing. We only want the best for you," she said.

Robert was now smoldering with red hot intensity. One of his eyes twitched every few seconds.

"I'll say this. You won't be living here if you go against our wishes. Get yourself together. Are you on drugs or something? What is the matter with you?" cried Robert.

I better throw them a bone. I gotta get outta here.

"Listen, I'll do some checking around and see what I can find out. I don't want you guys so mad at me. Okay?"

Leona smiled and relaxed her hands on the table.

"That's wonderful, honey. It's settled then." she said.

"Every two weeks I want status on this. Don't feed us a line of bull either. You don't want me any more pissed off than I already am. Now get out before I do something I will, I mean your mother will, regret." said Robert.

Colt picked up his coffee with two scones and exited the room in haste. *Dude, he was ready to tangle. I don't want to see him like that again.*

~~~

After the talk, Colt escaped by driving in the pouring rain. When it stopped raining, he felt better, as he always did. Everything was fresh and clean. It was if the world was purged of all unpleasantness. *Now I can get going again. That was no way to wake up.* It was early afternoon when he returned home. Leona was waiting for him when he stepped into the house. She looked worried.

"Colt, are you alright? Were we too hard on you?"

"I'm okay, I guess. Dad was pretty mad."

"You know we only want the best for you. I love you so much, honey."

Leona started to cry softly.

Colt hugged her and said, "I know you love me. This'll work out. I'll see what I can find out about college."

"So, you're okay now?"

"I feel a lot better. I just had to get away for a bit and clear my head."

After composing herself, Leona smiled and said, "I have a surprise for you."

"What's that?"

Colt would reserve judgment until he knew what this was about.

"You know Alison Monroe. She's having a problem with her stupid old computer. I told her you could help. Isn't that great?"

"Yeah, I'd be happy to help. Did she say what the problem was?"

"Something about email files or a network something. I don't understand all that computer lingo."

"Give me her number and I'll set up an appointment." said Colt with a smile.

"Just remember that she's going through a rough time. She just got divorced. So, you be extra nice. Wear something bright and colorful like you do. Maybe that will cheer her up."

"Okay Mom. I'll be extra nice to her."

Chapter 10

------Email-------
From: Monroe, Alison[AMonroe@aol.com]
To: Wise, Deborah[DebbieW@aol.com]
Subject: It's sooooo hard

Hi Deb
This breakup is soooo hard. He just left and acted like we were
never even married. I gave everything and what do I have?
At least all the papers are signed now. But how am I going to
start over. I feel so alone. And, I really miss being CLOSE!!!!
After all I'm not a teenager anymore. Maybe I can do to him
what he's done to me and find some young pretty thing. Ohhh,
did I really say that? I just don't know if anybody would want
me now? I'm just so sad and so tired of feeling unloved.

Please write
Ali

------Email-------

Colt's cell phone crackled with a high-pitched ring tone,
mimicking the Beatles song "Help". *An emergency? This is great.*
Now I can do something that won't make me fall asleep. The melodic
sound was an SOS. Colt had been periodically dozing off in class
and needed something to break the monotony. Now, he could
look forward to finishing the day doing something interesting,
something he loved. Also, he thought of later that evening when
he had an appointment with his mother's friend, Alison Monroe.
He 'd followed his mother's suggestion and was wearing bright,
loud apparel. He became enthused and energized when first
hearing the phone and was getting up in anticipation of making a

quick exit. *I have on my power clothes, too,* he thought. *I'm ready for anything.*

Colt answered, "Yo, this is Colt."

"This is Bobby. I have a box that won't come up. I've tried everything."

"Where are you at?" asked Colt.

"I'm at the district office. Can you come over?"

"I'll be there in ten. You saved me from falling asleep again in this class, which is a total waste of time."

Colt worked with Bobby for hours. They attempted to fix the personal computer using a variety of techniques, both simple and complex. Finally, Colt pulled out a CD and inserted it into the misbehaving box. He turned the computer off and then on again after a few minutes. A message displayed on the screen asking the question, *Do you want to Repair or Reinstall Microsoft Windows Millennium Edition?* Colt clicked in the checkbox next to "Reinstall" and then clicked on the "Continue" button. Lines of text moved up the screen while a flashing green light and a low-pitched whirring noise indicated that files were being copied to the hard disk.

"Man, computers sure can be hard to fix," said Bobby.

"Totally, dude! We tried everything we could think and got no love. Now with the OS and applications, it will take hours to reload," said Colt.

"I'm so sick of working on this thing. I know they're gonna be mad because all of their data is gone," whined Bobby.

"We had no choice. Reinstalling was the only thing we could do. Maybe they made backups. You never know." said Colt.

After another two hours the computer was up and running again. Both teenagers were drained from the ordeal and wanted to get home to relax. Colt didn't feel as bright or optimistic as he had earlier in the day. *I'm ready to forget about computers for a while. Just some food, TV and crash. I need to forget about this day.*

"I've had enough. Later dude," said Colt.

"Thanks Colt. You bailed me out again. See you later," said Bobby.

"Nobody saved anybody. We worked on it together and the computer won. Take it easy, bud."

~~~

Colt got into his old purple VW bug and zoomed off. *I'm sure glad this day's over.* The little round car sped south, out of Burien toward home. As he turned the corner and down the hill into Normandy Park, a very different and unusual thing happened. *What's that smell? I like it but where's it coming from?* A foreign scent like a strong perfume permeated his car. It's delicate aroma was intoxicating. *There's no way this is happening. It didn't smell like this when I got in. I must be going nuts.* The smell would not go away even when he rolled down the window and poked his head out. Colt stopped the car and looked around for the source of the exotic scent, but found nothing. He closed his eyes to gain his composure and figure out why he was sitting in the middle of a perfume mist. *Whoa, something changed. What is that?* Colt felt like he had entered a dream, but knew he was wide awake. In front of him was a familiar sight. A bank of bright, gray, hazy fog obscured a hidden sun. Scintillating violet specks appeared in various areas of the fog making it seem electric. *But I've always seen this in a dream.* He lost all feeling of being in his body as the sun pulled him forward like a huge magnet.

He moved toward the fog as if he was lying on top of a glider. When he neared the fog, Colt attempted to touch it, but found himself back in his body. *Crap, I'm back. Damn it. I almost got past the fog this time. I know there's a sun behind there. I need to see it.*

Once the waking dream ended, Colt sensed a memory tugging at him. *I know I forgot something, but what? I got so into that computer deal that I can't remember what it was.* After wracking his brain for some time, he finally remembered the appointment with his mothers' friend, Alison Monroe. His irritation turned into anger when he looked at his watch and saw that it read 7:12 p.m.

"Damn it," he muttered.

I was supposed to be there at 7:00! I hate forgetting appointments and being late. After the stressful day, Colt didn't want to deal with another broken computer. After weighing his options and thinking about his reception when he got home, he decided what to do. *Mom will be upset if I don't do this. I better just drop in on her friend and take a look.* Alison's house was not far away, which also helped him make the decision to head in that direction. *Maybe it will be easy. It can't be as bad as the last one.* When Colt arrived at Alison Monroe's house he remembered how pleasant she had sounded on the phone. *I wonder what she looks like.* He walked to the front door of the small, light green, one-story house that faced the Puget Sound. His cell phone rang just as he pushed the doorbell. Colt turned away from the door as he answered the call.

"Hello, this is Colt."

"Honey, this is your mother. Ali called and said you hadn't shown up. Is everything alright?"

"It's okay. I'm at her front door now. I gotta go. I'll see you later."

"Bye sweetie."

Colt was startled by the door opening behind him. When he turned, warm scented air enveloped him. He became slightly disoriented when he recognized the same potent, exotic scent from the earlier incident in his car. *Man, is it me smelling that or is it real?* After a moment he decided that it was something coming from the house. *Déjà vu or something, I guess. I'll figure it out later.* The strange event was weird and interesting, but would have to wait. He had work to do.

An attractive, trim, thirty-something woman stood facing him. She was shorter than he was by about four inches. Friendly brown eyes twinkled above a confident smile. Her hair, like his, was jet black and cut very short, giving her a youthful appearance.

"I'm so happy you made it. I know you'll save me from my computer," she said.

Colt slowly recovered his composure and noticed the rest of Alison Monroe's appearance. She wore a bright pink mini-skirt with a white silk blouse. He could not ignore that she was braless. The outlines of her small breasts were displayed clearly beneath the clinging silk. She held a glass of white wine in her hand. The entire scene stimulated all of Colt's senses in such a way that he felt himself being drawn into the house. It was warm and inviting.

"Hi, I'm Alison. Are you okay?"

"Er, uh, yeah. I've just had a long day, that's all. I guess you know that I'm Colt."

She smiled while putting her hand softly on his shoulder.

"Your clothes gave you away, Colt. Come in. Sit for a little while and relax. You probably need a break."

As he followed her into the house, Colt felt the pangs of desire starting to sneak into his tired mind. Alison Monroe was very friendly. She didn't treat him like a high school senior, which caught him off-guard. Also, the see-thru blouse was difficult to ignore. Only the fresh memory of his mother and her concern for her friend enabled him to keep desire at bay. He knew from experience that resisting sexual desire was an internal battle that was hard to win. As he followed her into a den, he said to himself, *I have to fix the computer and get out of here fast before I do something stupid.*

"Here's the computer. I lost some emails and I can't find some other things. Don't work on it yet, though. Wait a few minutes. I'll be right back. I know just the thing to help you relax after a long day." said Alison.

Colt was in no shape to argue as he struggled to wrap his erotic desires into a tidy controllable package. It was like pulling an anvil at the end of some twine. The anvil was winning the battle.

"Yeah, sure." answered Colt as he slumped into a chair in front of a desk. Alison returned holding two glasses of white wine. She handed one glass to Colt.

"Here's a toast to relaxation and a tech guru to fix all my problems," said Alison with a smile.

She touched his glass with hers and looked directly into his eyes. She was acting like they were old friends and treated Colt as an equal. *I wonder if I should drink this. She's probably right. I'll relax and be able to do the work better.* With the first sip of the sweet wine, Colt felt tension fading away. After not eating anything since lunch, he had little resistance to the alcohol. They both continued to sip the wine while they talked. The first topic of conversation was the problems with her computer. But, soon they were discussing their personal lives. Time flew by as the sweet wine took effect. Alison described being alone after her divorce and the difficulty in adjusting.

"After years of being together, my whole life has been turned upside down. I'm probably going to have to get a job. I don't mind working but it's been years since I've done it."

"I broke up with my girlfriend not too long ago. I have a hard time understanding girls. It's like they want to control everything," said Colt.

Alison was now very relaxed. Any formality that she had displayed earlier had disappeared. She talked to Colt with open friendliness.

"I think you need to meet a more mature woman who knows how to treat a man. Young girls are so emotional. After all, you aren't a little kid anymore. You have grown-up needs. I can see that."

Now sipping his second glass of wine on an empty stomach, Colt was tipsy. He found that everything Alison said to him made perfect sense. *Wow, she's so logical. She really understands me.* His feelings of frustration from earlier in the day and evening were giving way to a strong sense of egoistic, well-being. Computer problems, his mother, and other distracting feelings were erased by a growing bubble of happiness. He loved talking with this friendly, understanding woman in her pleasant little home.

Then, in an instant, Alison was crying! It was a soft, muffled sobbing with tears streaming down her cheeks, causing her makeup to streak. Colt was afraid that he must have done something wrong. *I knew this was going way too well.*

"What's the matter? Is it something I said?"

"Oh, it's nothing. Nothing really," said Alison between convulsions.

"It must be something. I know that things have been hard for you."

"It's, it's just that after he left me, I stopped feeling pretty. I'm the ugliest thing in the world," she moaned.

Her small body shook with each sob.

"Don't think that way, Alison. I think you're more than pretty. You're beautiful."

After a few seconds of silence, Alison said, "Oh, thank you, Colt. You're so sweet. I'm really happy you're with me. If you hadn't been here I might have cried for hours. You make me feel like a woman again. I better go pull myself together. I'll be just a bit."

After about five minutes Alison returned with the half-full bottle of wine and poured until each of their glasses was full. Alison's blouse was now partially unbuttoned. She leaned toward Colt, who could not help staring at her breasts. Alison brightened as Colt stared with uninhibited desire. Slowly, with great effort, Colt lifted his gleaming eyes to hers.

"What is that smell? I sssorta like it." he asked.

"Oh, that's a scented candle. It's patchouli. Do you like it? I hear in India they use it to set the mood for romance."

Somewhere in the back of his mind Colt remembered something about that perfumed smell and his car, but could not grab onto the full memory. He was now intoxicated by Alison Monroe and her white wine.

"Uh, really? I never thought of that. Yeah, I really like it. This is really nice, being here with you, Alison," said Colt.

Alison snaked closer to Colt, allowing another blouse button to come undone.

"You know, I think it's time that you call me Ali. This is wonderful for me, too. I love having you here. I really think we hit it off. Don't you?"

"It's like I've known you forever, Ali," said Colt.

Colt closed his eyes and took a large gulp of wine. When he opened them, Alison was sitting next to him with her hand lightly massaging his inner thigh. She stared into his eyes from a distance of a few feet. He could smell her musky perfume and hair. When he looked away from her eyes to stare at her breasts, his body involuntarily reacted. What might have bothered him earlier in the evening now seemed perfectly normal. He had an overwhelming urge to kiss her, even though somewhere in the back of his mind a voice echoed caution. It was like a tiny drop of water hitting the bottom of a deep well. The message being sent was never received through the wall of intoxication. As he moved toward her hypnotic eyes to express his desire, Alison grasped his hand firmly and stood up, brushing one of her now-exposed breasts against his face.

"Come with me, my young prince."

"Whatever you want, Ali, whatever you want."

Chapter 11

------Email-------
From: Jones, Bobby[Bobbyj@yahoo.com]
To: O'Brien, Colt[ColtOB@yahoo.com]
Subject: Big meeting

Hey Colt
i herd there's gonna be a meeting about that new computer deal. Its sat
morn at 10 at the swedens. Lets check it out. Call me.

   Bobby

------Email-------

Frigid waves of rain rolled in from the Puget Sound, hitting
the purple VW bug as it wound its way through Burien's back
streets. Bobby Jones sat next to Colt who was driving.

"Dude, we're almost there. I know this has gotta be some
scam," said Colt.

"I guess we'll find out," answered Bobby.

The little car pulled up and parked in front of the Sweden
home, which was perched on a hill overlooking the water. Colt
and Bobby, who were bundled in warm coats, jumped out and
dashed for the front door. Ron Sweden met them with a
pleasant smile.

"You came at a good time. We're about to start. I'm Ron
Sweden. It's great to see you guys."

"Hi Mr. Sweden. I'm Colt O'Brien and this is my friend
Bobby Jones."

"I thought it might be you guys. Mr. Towne said you might show up. He spoke highly of both of you. Come in and find a seat."

The first thing that Colt noticed as the boys entered the open, warm living room, was a large white board covered with black scribbles. *Looks like more mumbo jumbo to me,* thought Colt. About 20 adults and teenagers were sitting facing the board, talking amongst themselves. The room was buzzing with an aura of anticipation. The smell of strong coffee permeated the air, adding to the electric atmosphere.

Colt scanned the entire room, soaking everything in. He tried to sense the aura created by the people in the room.

"I wonder what they did with the furniture. Now it's a classroom or something. I need some of that coffee. It smells like Starbucks."

"Man, you read my mind. That coffee smells great," said Bobby.

Both tech-savvy teenagers arrived in a skeptical mood, but were now feeling a sense of excitement along with the others.

"Man, there's some juice in this room. Way different," whispered Bobby.

"Yeah, these people seem jacked up for this thing. Now, that's not something I've ever seen before," said Colt.

"And it's not just kids. Parents are here too."

Ron Sweden walked to the front of the room and started to erase the scribbles on the white board. Everyone stopped talking and focused on the tall slender man. He was the only person in the room who wore a suit and tie. He turned to face the audience and closed his eyes, clasped his hands together and stretched them with palms facing the audience. After a few moments he smiled, making eye contact with each member of the audience.

65

Ron Sweden started speaking as if he was breathing fresh spring air on a sunny day after a long storm. He was relaxed, but in total command of his words and movements. He wrapped the audience in a blanket of sunny optimism with no apparent effort.

"This is an important day. You've all been invited here to discover a new learning adventure. You might ask, 'What is this all about?' It's about three things. It's about opportunity. It's about hard work. And, it's about achieving something."

His refined hand gestures gave physical impact to his words. "I've been asked why I'm doing this. I have to admit, I'm selfish. I do it for my son, for his education. I can't think of a better reason."

A hand was raised by a man who seemed to be the father of the skinny, pimply-faced boy sitting next to him.

"Why are we here if you're doing this for your kid?" asked the man.

"Mr. Carbon and I were approached by our sons to help them become Microsoft Certified Professionals. By passing one exam, both Billy and Gunner have achieved that. Now the bar has been set higher. They want to achieve more. Each of you can do the same."

I don't even agree with him and I'm halfway convinced, thought Colt. He whispered in Bobby's ear, "He can't fool me. I know there's a trick in there somewhere."

Ron Sweden continued explaining the program. He had command of his audience, including Colt and Bobby, throughout his presentation.

He ended by saying, "You have a chance to do something unique, something special. Oh yes, you'll work hard, but remember the benefits. Thanks for attending. Now Billy and Gunnar will give a demonstration of what they've learned."

Colt had been wondering how these parents convinced Mr. Towne to agree to have this program at Highline. *I think this guy hypnotized Mr. Towne. A lot of this has to be made up. It sounds way too good to be true.* As Colt struggled between his belief that the new program was a fraud and his attraction to the challenge, Billy and Gunnar walked toward the white board. *Okay, now we'll see what the little nerds really know. Probably not that much*, thought Colt

"Hi, I'm Billy Carbon. One of the tests is called NT Server. We're going to talk about how memory works and different modes."

Both boys wrote diagrams and key words on the white board as they talked about how the Microsoft NT operating system functioned. *Dude, this is technical stuff. Creepy. Hell, I don't even know if it's for real*, thought Colt. When the subject of User Mode and Kernel Mode was presented, Colt, Bobby, and the entire audience seemed to deflate. Colt considered himself to be very knowledgeable about computer operating systems but he didn't understand any of it. He waved his hand back and forth in frustration.

"Hi, I'm Colt O'Brien. I've done a lot with Windows computers and never had to know this stuff. How does this help anyone fix computers?"

Gunnar Sweden looking a little nervous tried to compose himself. After a pause he answered.

"There are a lot of things in the tests that you won't use much. You still have to learn it, though. We know more than we ever thought we could and we just started."

"So why do it if it's like that? What good is it?" said Colt.

Ron Sweden interrupted as he looked directly at Colt.

"If you want to be a professional, you should be able to pass the exams. If you want respect, you now have an opportunity to show what you know,"

Damn, he cut me off. He's calling me out.

The boys continued talking for about ten minutes and then summed up the material. There was light applause from the stunned audience that brought smiles to the young teenagers' cherubic faces.

Now another man was facing the audience. He wore a beige baseball cap with the word "Microsoft" across the front. Unlike Ron Sweden, he was dressed in a t-shirt and faded blue jeans.

"Hello, my name is Matthew Carbon. I'm helping with curriculum and teaching classes for the program. Since we've all been sitting and listening for some time, I'll be brief. You'll pass one exam to become a Microsoft Certified Professional. To become a Microsoft Certified Systems Engineer, you'll need to pass five more for a total of six. The exams are pass/fail. These certifications are usually earned by people who are already working in the computer industry. So, for a student in high school to earn one of the certifications is very special."

Matthew wrote items on the white board.

Books
Classes
Coaching
Practice tests
Hands on practice
Assessments
Students helping students

He then talked about each category in a very direct, confident way. It was very easy for the entire audience to understand the simple outline. Every person in the room could see that the plan would work. They all understood that the key element were effort and dedication. After about twenty minutes, he ended the talk.

"As you can see, this is about learning the material inside and out. The exams are purposely made difficult and it's win or lose, with no in between. Someone asked why he should do this earlier. To me, the main reason is that it's not easy. If you do this, you've achieved something. This isn't about sitting in a classroom for an hour each day; it's about doing whatever it takes to pass the exams. We'll help every student do that, but there are no shortcuts. Thanks for listening. Mr. Sweden, the boys and I will be available for questions."

"Can you believe that Sweden challenged me? That other guy, too. Can you believe that?" said Colt to Bobby.

"Man, there's no way I'm working that hard for some useless certification," said Bobby.

Colt was agitated. He was beginning to feel that the exams had to be as hard as advertised. However, he still didn't understand how Billy and Gunnar were passing the tests.

"If those punk kids can do it, so can I," he said.

"Wow, really? Don't you have better things to do, Colt?" said Bobby.

"It pisses me off that those twerps have the cert and I don't. That Sweden guy acted like I couldn't pass one test. I want to show him that those kids aren't any smarter than me."

Bobby smiled, but tried not to show it.

"Go for it. You can tell me how easy it is when you pass one of those tests."

Chapter 12

------Email-------
From: O'Brien, Colt[ColtOB@yahoo.com]
To: Jones, Bobby[bobbyj@yahoo.com]
Subject: lets check it out
----

im still thinking about joining the geeker thing / that guy got me
riled up / maybe I can figure out how to pass like the little twerps
colt

------Email-------

    The two friends sat in the main dining area at a tiny table in their favorite eating establishment, Dave's Diner. It was lunchtime and the small room was filled with customers. The aroma of fried burgers and fries wafted through the air. Colt was noticeable in the drab crowd because of the bright red jacket that he was wearing. Next to Bobby, in his rather plain attire, he looked like a neon light on a Las Vegas strip. Their food had been eaten, but the young men continued to talk while sipping on sodas. A flicker of curiosity flashed across the face of Bobby as Colt attempted to hammer home a point. Colt leaned forward in his chair while clenching and un-clenching his hands. His whole body was tense like a cornered animal that was ready to pounce or run.

    "Those twerps can't outdo me. I just don't think the cert thing is that hard," said Colt.

    Bobby leaned back in his undersized chair. He was enjoying his friend's intensity. He always became amused when Colt was agitated. And, this new happening in the computer landscape of

Highline High had Colt more irritated that Bobby had seen in a long time.

"You're just mad because now people are thinking that those kids are really savvy. Heck, you'll be gone soon anyway. Why do you care?" said Bobby.

"I don't like people to act like I'm a loser. That guy looked me straight in the eye and as much as said that I couldn't do it. I say screw them all."

Bobby baited his friend, who was building up to an explosion.

"All he was saying was if you're good, then show it by passing the test."

"We both know that I can pass the stupid test," yelled Colt.

Customers at other tables looked up at the young men. Bobby put a finger to his lips to quiet Colt down. He had to control himself to not burst out laughing at his friend's temper tantrum. Bobby lowered his voice.

"I don't think you have time to mess with this stuff. Also, I noticed that you aren't seeing chicks much. That's unusual for you."

"Hey dude, don't worry about my love life. Chicks can be more hassle than they're worth sometimes. I needed a break."

Colt thought about his visit to Alison Monroe's house and the hangover he had the next day. He didn't know whether to be happy or mad. Although his ego told him he had been a real man, most of the night and the drive home was a blur. That made him angry. Colt didn't like to be inebriated or forgetful. And, driving while intoxicated made him feel ashamed. *I won't be a stupid, dumb, sleepwalking zombie. And no way am I going to run over someone because I'm drunk.*

Bobby interrupted Colt's inner world.

"What about college and fixing PCs?"

"I've talked enough about it. I'm going to do this. Mr. Carbon will tell me how to get started. That other guy didn't think I could measure up. I'll deal with someone I like." said Colt.

Now that he had decided his plan of attack, he relaxed a little and smiled.

"Okay man, okay. I see you're into this no matter what I say," said Bobby.

"When was it ever any other way?" asked Colt.

Colt grinned and patted his friend on the back as they walked into the drizzly afternoon.

~~~

Billy Carbon looked up from a large computer screen and answered the ringing phone in his basement bedroom.

"Hello."

"Hi, this is Colt O'Brien. Is your dad there?"

"Yeah, hang on." Billy walked over the stairs and yelled. "Hey Dad, pick up the phone,"

Matthew Carbon, who was on the main floor of the house, came on the line.

"Hello, this is Matthew."

"Hi, Mr. Carbon. This is Colt O'Brien. We met at the Sweden's house."

"Oh, hello Colt. What's up? Can I help you with something?" asked Matthew.

"I had some more questions about the certification stuff."

"Fire away."

"How long does it take?"

"It depends on a lot of things. We expect to see two months of study for the first exam."

"Is that how long Billy and Gunnar took?"

"Yes, but they study for about a month for each exam now."

"I know there's a trick to this. What is it?"

"It's like we said in the meeting. You work your tail off. I'll tell you right now, if you don't want to work, then don't do it. Mostly, you read. If you stick to it, your reading comprehension will go sky high," said Matthew.

"Do you have the stuff, like books?" asked Colt.

"We have enough materials to get you going. The Sweden's have more than we do here, but you can start with a few books."

"Can I stop by and get started?"

"Sure, come over. What about your friend? Is he interested?"

"I don't think so, but I'll bring him along."

"We live in Seahurst. Do you know where our house is?"

"Uh, I think so. It's the purple house, right?"

"That's it, Colt."

"We'll be over in about ten minutes," said Colt.

"We'll see you then," said Matthew.

Colt and Bobby stood in front of the Carbon house. They stared up at a lilac-colored two-story edifice with dark blue trim. The sun had peeked out from the gray clouds making the structure stand out. The house seemed to be glowing while everything around it seemed drab. Colt and Bobby were hypnotized.

"Man, what a color. Now I know why everybody says to find the purple house in Seahurst. No way anybody could miss that," said Bobby.

Colt was feeling serene. A wave of well-being emanated outward from the house into him. It caused him to feel extremely cheerful. It was a strange, foreign feeling that came over him; not something he had ever experienced. He felt that this powerful force should be pulling him in, but the presence of the home was not demanding, only uplifting. Colt sensed that even if he stood in place, the power of the purple house would stay as strong as if he were inside.

"Yeah dude. I'm feeling some good vibes. I think I'll like this." said Colt.

Bobby tapped Colt's arm and started to stroll toward the front door. The boys walked up the driveway to the front porch. The door was opened by Billy Carbon before Bobby could knock.

"Hey guys, come on in. My dad is here," said Billy.

As they walked into the living room, Colt saw that the ceiling was painted with clouds. He was overcome with a strong sense of being elevated above the floor. *This must be what walking on air feels like,* he thought.

"Hi guys, find a seat," said Matthew Carbon.

The two young men sat on a plush, antique sofa and looked around. The living room was just as unusual as the outside of the house. Old framed prints and antique furniture filled the entire room. The walls were a rose color. Nothing modern, or what they thought of as normal, could be seen, except for the overstuffed, brown leather chair that Matthew Carbon sat in. There was no television in sight. Both Bobby and Colt felt like they had stepped into the past; a past of beauty, substance and serenity. The teenagers melted into this inviting environment. They were entranced by the aura of the room and curious about it. Colt could feel a deep, delicate, bubble of energy building within him. It radiated out in all directions.

"Wow, this is a neat house," said Bobby.

"You can give credit to my wife. It's all her doing," smiled Matthew.

"She must be really different, in a good way, I mean. I've never seen anything like this," said Colt.

"I try to stay out of her way. Everybody notices that she has a creative streak," said Matthew.

"Please tell her we like your house," said Bobby.

"I'll do that. Now let's get down to business. Is it just going to be Colt trying this or both of you?"

"Just me. Bobby isn't ready yet." said Colt with a little bit of pride.

"Billy, give Colt the books. Colt, you should read the yellow book first and then the other one. If you get through those, let me know and I'll give you some other things to do," said Matthew.

Colt looked at the books. I spite of his overall sense of well-being, he frowned as he turned the pages of the yellow book.

"It says this book is for dummies. I'm no dummy," said Colt.

"Don't worry about the title. We know what we're doing. Just start out with the easy stuff and work up to the harder stuff. And believe me when I say that some of the material you will go over if very complex.

"Okay, I'll do what you say. Thanks," said Colt.

"Is that it? No more questions?" said Matthew Carbon.

No way I want to leave yet. This place is too mellow, thought Colt. He was floating on a cushion of wispy, friendly, pillow-like clouds. His usual drive to move forward without relaxing had been temporarily suspended. Inner batteries, unknown to him, were now recharging. He was reminded of Thanksgiving when his mother asked him to baste the turkey. He was now soaking up energy like the empty tube sucking up turkey juices. Colt talked for about twenty minutes more. He was not conscious in the usual sense, but felt extremely relaxed. Words only came out of his mouth to delay his departure. His main goal was to remain in this field of pleasantness as long as possible. He craved the healing vibrations of the Carbon house. After a time, Bobby became restless.

"I think we should be going," said Bobby.

"Oh yeah, I guess we should," said Colt.

"Remember that it's hard work that will make the difference, Colt," said Matthew.

"Thanks Mr. Carbon," said both young men.

Outside, they stopped to look at the house one last time.

"Man, our mothers won't believe this place. How can we begin to describe it?" said Bobby.

"Yeah, that was really different. It was outer space in there," said Colt.

"I could tell. Man, you were not yourself. You totally mellowed out."

"Yeah, I guess I did, Dude," said Colt. "I guess I did."

After Colt and Bobby left, Matthew Carbon's wife Elyce, entered the room. She was petite with sea-blue eyes and deep red hair. She stood in front of Matthew.

"Who was the young man with the black hair?" she asked with a curious glint in her eyes.

"That was Colt O'Brien. He's going to try for the certification like Billy."

"I could feel his aura all the way upstairs. It was very strong."

"Well, he's usually a bit high strung, but he sat right there on that couch and really relaxed. I was wondering if he was ever going to leave." said Matthew.

"I think that young man is in for more that he knows. I hope he listens to his inner voice. I fear that he acts before he thinks," said Elyce.

"Well honey, you know about that inner stuff. I don't know how you see it, but I'm a believer," said Matthew.

"He has some special talents. But, I wonder if he'll learn how to use those talents and not be hurt by them."

"I hope the young man succeeds, sweetheart. He has some spunk. But you're right. He has a reputation of acting before thinking."

She closed her eyes and became very still.

"I pray that he does find his way. It will not be easy," she said.

Chapter 13

------Email-------
From: Sweden, Gunnar[gunman@yahoo.com]
To: Carbon, Billy[billg@hocs.biz]
Subject: fun - we make up
----

hey billgee
 dad askd for us to thnk up fun stuff. lets hav piza in the hole
we can figger somthin out.

gunman

------Email-------

The hole was ripe with aromas of a hot pepperoni pizza. Billy Carbon's basement bedroom, known as the hole, had little ventilation and no windows. Cool cement walls surrounded Billy and Gunnar, who were sitting on an old sofa. The boys were surrounded by teenage messiness, the exact opposite of the organized elegance on display above them on the main floor of the house. Neither of them spoke while wolfing down steaming pizza. Overcoming hunger was their primary focus. Billy had a favorite frozen, rising-crust pizza that he embellished with extra assorted cheeses. It was the only thing he cooked and he was always proud of the result.

A sci-fi video was playing on the large televison. Sounds from the movie were booming from hidden speakers making it difficult to talk or to think. Billy saw movement out of the corner of his left eye. He looked to see his father waving an arm from the foot of the stairs. He looked serious. His lips were moving, but Billy could not hear what he was saying. He jumped up and turned down the volume.

"Yeah Dad?" said Billy.

"Hey, keep it down. You don't need to shake the house. Your mother is afraid that windows will start breaking," said Matthew Carbon.

"Okay Dad. It wasn't that bad, was it?"

"Yes, yes, yes! It was that bad. Keep it down. I thought you guys were studying or something?"

"Hi, Mr. Carbon. We're going to think up fun ideas for the program. We're watching a movie while we eat. It's about time for us to talk anyway," said Gunnar.

"The parents of the world will be pleased. See you later," said Matthew.

Billy turned off the TV and the two boys continued working on their assignment. The mission was to think up fun, cool activities for students in the program. Ron Sweden had told them that with all of the hard study, the group needed to let off some steam, too.

Before eating, the ideas had flowed freely. Now it was time for each of them to pick a favorite activity to suggest to Ron Sweden. Billy moved over to the computer and opened a list of ideas. Both boys had typed in about five items. Billy looked at Gunnar and spoke.

"Hey bud, we need to decide on the best activities. Let's finish this."

"Uh, sure, whatever. I told you all my ideas," said Gunnar.

"We need to pick our favorites. Your dad said to pick one each for now," said Billy.

"Hey, I like the LAN party idea," said Gunnar.

They had both been to exactly one LAN party and had been enthralled. Gunnar was apt to tell anyone who would listen how awesome it was killing pixilated foes in the darkness with rock music reverberating around them. Neither had known, at the time, that it was possible to connect multiple computers together and play games. Although the party consisted of just five computers, with players on each, it opened up a multitude of possibilities for them. The sense of immersion had been complete. Each had lost all sense of place and time. It was the best experience of their young lives.

Billy's eyes widened as he remembered how much fun they had. It was the second favorite thing to do on his list.

"It'll be fantastic. We'll need to have food, lots of computers, and gamers cranking on them. What a blast that will be," said Billy.

"What's your favorite idea?" said Gunnar.

Gunnar thought he already knew the answer to the question. Billy had always wanted to go to the Microsoft campus in Redmond, Washington. His dream was to meet the Microsoft legend Bill Gates.

With a wistful look, Billy spoke.

"Microsoft, baby. That's the best idea. We can see where it all happens. Just think how much they affect everything. Man, that would be awesome. Maybe we could see Bill Gates walking around checking code."

"No way he checks code anymore. He has master coders to do that. He's way beyond that stuff," said Gunnar.

"I heard he used to look at code all the time. I guess maybe he goes to meetings and stuff now."

"I think my dad wants to go there even more than you do. He's already calling everybody he can to set up something," said Gunnar.

"I really hope he gets us in. And, I hear they have a store where they give huge discounts on software. Totally cool," said Billy.

The young teens went back to watching TV while thinking about future possibilities.

~~~

Ron Sweden dialed and put the thin, silver cell phone to his ear. He looked hopeful and focused while waiting for an answer.

"Hi, this is Ron Sweden. Is this Dick Hansen?"

"Yes, this is Dick. Hi, Ron. My wife told me that you would call. How can I help you? She said you were pretty wound up about something Microsoft related."

"Mr. Carbon and I have started a Microsoft networking program at Highline High School. The program is doing very well and the kids are achieving great things. We thought our success would open doors at Microsoft, since we are using their certification program as the basis of our study. However, so far we haven't really connected with the right folks over there. I'm looking for help with opening up the lines of communication."

Ron waited with trepidation, hoping that he finally had found the right person to lubricate the red tape train that seemed to be stalling his attempts.

"I guess you're finding out that Microsoft deals with everybody in the world and filters are in place to protect the company. When you want to talk to someone in charge, it can get very frustrating. What exactly did you want to do?"

"We have about ten kids, with more joining each day. They're passing the Microsoft certification exams. Most of them are only high school freshmen. We thought it would be great for the kids to experience the Redmond campus environment. It would be a field trip, but we want it to be about achievement and future careers, too."

"I'm surprised that you guys were able to start something like this and keep it going. So, you guys are sponsored by the school?" said Dick Hansen with a bit of admiration in his voice.

"Yes, they're happy with our progress. Mr. Towne, the principal, is singing our praises to all who will listen. We're also part of the High Tech Learning Center which is for many schools."

"I've been with Microsoft for many years. I know who the right people are to contact and the best approach. We really do support this type of educational activity, but we need to know who we're dealing with. I'll see what I can find out. It sounds like you guys are doing great things."

For the first time during the call, Ron relaxed. He knew that he'd found the pathway into Microsoft.

"Finally, I have someone who can help. This is really great. Thanks Dick."

"I'm interested in hearing more. Would you like to meet for lunch sometime?

"Definitely, let's do it. Just tell me what works best for you."

Ron Sweden pushed the button on his cell phone and grinned. Visions of the coveted field trip danced in his head.

Chapter 14

------Email-------
From: Carbon, Billy[billg@hocs.biz]
To: Sweden, Gunnar[gunman@yahoo.com]
Subject: flash

```
gunman
flash was just here. he took some books. his
bud didn't want in. i wonder how flash will do. it
won't be long til we kno

billg
```

------Email-------

Colt sat staring at the two books and frowned. *Oh man, this is looking so un-cool. It feels like boring work and I haven't even started yet.* He was a good student, if not an accomplished one. However, senior year he had taken a vacation from school work and he knew it. The credits he needed to graduate were already accounted for and he had not studied all year. His plan was to cruise through until he got his diploma and then to turn his back on school forever. *How did I get myself into this? I don't want to read more books and be bored beyond belief. I don't even care about school stuff anymore.* Then, he thought of the two smiling freshmen who were already in the limelight. In his mind, they were constantly being praised by parents and teachers. *I can't stand that the whole school thinks those punks are more technical than I am.* Most of all, he knew that they would be the ones who were called when a computer wasn't working. *I'm the go-to guy, not them. I should be the*

83

first to be called and not those punks. Colt was now feeling uneasy about jumping into this new arena. He felt a sharp tightening in the pit of his stomach. Doubt was slipping into tiny cracks of his confidence. *No way I'm going to let fear control me. No way do I back down from this. Once in, I'm in all the way.* Colt was determined to push ahead in spite of the vision of a enormous, white-capped mountain that was looming over him. *It's going to be like climbing up Mount Rainier.*

The yellow soft-cover book sitting on the desk challenged Colt in silence. He read the title to himself: MCSE Windows NT Workstation 4 for Dummies Training Kit. The book was less than half the size of the other book that was also sitting on the table. He hated that it had the word "Dummies" in the title and felt that he was given that particular book to send him a message: Colt O'Brien was not smart enough; he was stupid. He grabbed the book and threw it against the bedroom wall.

"Screw them all!" he yelled.

He looked at the other hardcover book wondering why it was so much bigger. The title was MCSE: NT Workstation 4 Study Guide. It seemed huge and intimidating. Even when he was doing his school work, he never would have opened a book like that. Hoping to see something recognizable in the table of contents, he scanned it. *I don't know about any of this crap and none of it looks interesting.* Colt found it difficult to connect what he was seeing to his experience with computers. Sensing that his resolve was slipping, he said to himself, *Stop screwing around. Do it or don't do it, now!* He picked up the yellow book from the floor and started to read it. *No turning back.*

The house was silent except for the occasional flurry of rain hitting the roof and windows. Colt stretched and yawned. He looked at the clock radio, which displayed the time. It was 2:30 a.m. Somehow, he had summoned the energy to read the entire dummies training kit book. *I don't think I'm supposed to feel more like a dummy than when I started. I thought I knew boring, but this is bad news.* The book covered facts that he had no interest in. He read every word, but his un-disciplined mind was thinking of other, more interesting things, most of the time. Fixing computers, hanging with Bobby Jones, movies, the web; all were far more enticing than learning Windows NT. Most of all was the constant distraction of girls and sex. Over and over he would return to his experience with Alison Monroe. The passing of time had allowed his ever-present libido to color his memories. Colt no longer remembered that he had been seduced with the aid of white wine or the headache he experienced all of the next day. He was not thinking about the consequences or that Alison was a friend of his mother's. Colt only remembered that he was a prince; he was desired. He remembered feeling like he was ten feet tall. *Hell, she told me I was a hero. I understand enough of this. I'm still the guy that can fix any computer.* Confidence replaced humility as optimism pushed reality into the background. *This stuff won't be that tough. I can do this crap.*

~~~

The sun was shining in Colt's face forcing him to open his eyes. He sat up on the bed and grabbed a pair of gray sweat pants that were on the floor. The clock displayed 1:08 p.m. It was Sunday and both of his parents were at home when he walked into the kitchen to make some coffee.

"Hi honey. This is late, even for you," said Leona while hugging him.

"I was studying. It's a new computer thing," said Colt.

"What computer thing? I thought we discussed this. You need to get serious about college and stop wasting time with computers," said Robert.

"Hey, Mr. Towne told me it'd be good for me to do it. So, I'm trying it out." answered Colt a little defensively.

Robert looked at his son with suspicion and irritation.

"How much time will it take? How will it help you get to college? Is the school running this?"

"Uh, sort of. Some parents are running it, but the school is involved. I think it'll take a lot of time. I'll have to take tough tests, I guess."

"Give me the names and numbers of the parents running this thing and I'll give them a call. I'll find out what is really happening."

"Robert, don't be so suspicious. Studying is good, isn't it? Colt, drink your coffee and don't worry about him. I think you're doing great," said Leona.

"Listen honey, we've trusted him too many times. I don't trust him anymore," said Robert.

"I know you'll do whatever you need to, dear, but I think Colt is doing fine. Didn't he say that the school sponsored this class? Colt, how did it go at Ali's house? Were you able to fix her computer?"

Colt went into a confused state of panic. *Crap. She would ask about that.* He took a sip of coffee while formulating what to say. Parts of the night at Ali's house flashed in and out of his mind. He sensed that his unsuspecting mother would not approve of the things that happened at her friend's house, in her friend's bedroom. With Leona asking questions, his confidence of the night before disappeared. *I better not talk about that night any more than I need to.*

86

"Her computer had a lot of problems. I'm going to have to go back over there. Uh, I'm glad you reminded me. I feel bad that I didn't get it done in one trip."

I think that was enough talking about Ali Monroe. Now I need to get outta here.

"She called and told me that you were great and that she's hoping you'll come back soon to finish the job. She said that you were really sweet to help her out."

Colt realized that he would actually have to see her again and decide how to proceed. Thinking about Alison Monroe was easy, but the idea that he would have to deal with the situation did not appeal to him at all.

"So she called, huh? I'll get over there as soon as I can, Mom," said Colt.

Colt knew it was time to get out of the kitchen, which was becoming very, very hot.

Chapter 15

------Email-------
From: O'Brien, Colt[ColtOB@yahoo.com]
To: Jones, Bobby[Bobbyj@yahoo.com]
Subject: We need to talk

Hey Bobinator

Chics man! They can sure screw up things.
My life is getting messy. Lets meet soon.

Colt

------Email-------

The conversation had been pleasant enough. Alison Monroe was prim and proper on the other end of the line. Nothing she said indicated that their previous encounter was anything more than a dedicated young man helping her with a difficult computer problem. While she talked about email and having her computer screen freeze up, Colt remembered parts of their last meeting in disjointed scenes that were sprinkled with lust, self-satisfaction and nervousness. *Dude, she got you drunk and did her thing. No way it was an accident.* Now that some time had passed and the name Ali" was voiced through his mother's lips, Colt was starting to have misgivings about the entire situation. Every time he thought of the events of that night, he saw his mother's face. Also, the feeling of not being in control still disturbed him. *She had me dangling like a stupid puppet. And, where will it end up? Where would I fit in?* He tried to use logic to understand what to expect from Alison. He came to the conclusion that if she had felt embarrassed by their first encounter, then she never would've asked him to come back. Even though Ali was acting like nothing had happened or would happen, his psychic radar detected covered pockets of emotion that he couldn't interpret. Although he sensed that she had a hidden agenda, he couldn't be sure. His psychic radar had malfunctioned many times before.

"I've been really busy lately. I'll need to get in and out quickly," said Colt.

"Oh, do you think you can fix it that fast, Colt?" asked Alison.

She sounds so sweet. It's like it's all a forgotten dream. Sorta like it never really happened.

"I think I know what the problem is. If I'm right, it shouldn't take longer than an hour."

"How about Tuesday night at eight? Will that be okay?"

Whatever, I better just get this over with.

"That should be fine," said Colt.

"I'll see you then, Colt."

~~~

The door opened and Colt looked at Alison. She was wearing tan slacks, sandals and a gray silk blouse. It seemed like it was his mother's friend in front of him and not a recent lover. He recalled the last time he stood at this door. Alison had not been wearing a bra and a strong, enticing, scent of patchouli was emanating from the house. *So far, so good. Maybe I can get through this without any hassles.* The environment seemed very tame and Colt was well-fed and rested. He sensed no tentacles of desire lashing out and pulling at him. *This is good. No romance vibes in the air. I don't need any temptation. This whole mistake has to end right now.* For Colt, it was over. He knew deep down that any more intimate contact with his mother's friend could only lead to trouble.

"Hello Colt, come in," said Alison with no hint of an ulterior motive.

Colt tried to stay neutral and distant.

"Hi, Alison."

"Do you want me to get you something, coffee, tea, or something stronger?"

"Tea will be fine. I need to concentrate on getting your computer fixed. I didn't get very far last time."

"Why don't you get started and I'll brew some tea."

Colt followed her into the house. *Well, that's out of the way. Maybe this will be no big deal.*

As he passed the kitchen, he noticed one full glass of white wine and one empty glass on the counter. He recalled the last time he had white wine in this house and felt a twinge in his gut along with a slight dizziness. *I'm just nervous. I need to work fast and stay away from the booze. Dude, don't start imagining things.*

When he reached the computer, Colt went through the same ritual that he always did. He opened his bag and removed the items that he would need to do his work. In this case those items were CDs and floppy disks that contained software applications and utilities. Next, he shut down the PC and restarted it. After a preliminary scan of the machine, he called to his employer.

"Is that tea almost ready? I have a few questions about your accounts and email," said Colt.

Alison entered the room and handed a large steaming mug to Colt. He set it on the desk and turned to her. Colt looked for any change in the mood of his hostess. She seemed relaxed, but nothing more. This allowed him to relax, also. *Home free, baby. This will soon be a memory.*

"Sure Colt. What questions do you have?" she said.

Colt wrote down information on a medium-sized yellow pad as Alison answered his questions. She was very pleasant and direct when responding. A delicate scent of perfume surrounded her. It was mixed with a distinct but faint odor of white wine. The smells distracted him, but soon he was able to re-focus on the work.

"Thanks. That's all I need for now. Let me work on this for awhile."

Alison smiled and held his gaze for a moment longer than before.

"Okay, Colt."

As she walked away, she brushed against Colt and her silk blouse made contact with his shoulder. It seemed innocent, but he sensed a slight jolt of electrical current arcing between them. *Whoa, what the hell was that?* Erotic visions entered his thoughts. Colt knew that if he had been drinking, even a small amount, he would be obsessing about how to get Ali Monroe into the bedroom. Instead of feeling concerned about being seduced by Alison, he was becoming concerned about his own self-control. *Just control yourself and stop worrying about her.*

Colt worked on the problems in front of him, hoping to move his attention into another area. After a short time, his lascivious thoughts subsided. He was able to fix one problem after another, which always pleased him and spurred him on. Alison's computer functioned better with each problem that he solved. After about forty minutes, Colt considered his job complete.

"Ali, I need about five more minutes to wrap this up."

"Can I bring anything in with me? Do you want more tea?"

"No thanks. I have to split," said Colt.

In what seemed to be a few seconds, Colt felt two supple hands on his shoulders, and the smell of perfume and wine from behind. The soft but firm hands were massaging his shoulders in a sensuous, persistent way. In an instant, he was physically aroused. Unlike the last time, he had the self-control to resist her obvious intentions. Colt moved her hands and stood up. She had a look of unbridled desire in her sparkling brown eyes above pouty lips and bright pink cheeks.

Colt was struggling to resist her obvious intentions.

"Um, uh, er, I don't want to do anything I will regret," he blurted out.

Ali was moving a hand toward Colt's mid-section.

"Baby, it was so good with us. I need you and I know you need me, too."

"I need to leave," said Colt as he backed away.

"I can see you're ready for me, baby, really ready. Oh Colt, let's just do it one more time."

Colt could feel her desire sapping his last reserves of self-control. He turned and gathered up his disks, threw them in his bag and turned for the door. He was now rushing like he was about to be pulled into quicksand.

"I have to go. I have to go now."

Alison's eyes flashed with anger as her petite body tensed. Her fingers clenched into fists.

"So Colt, you just use me and then leave? Am I only good for one night?"

Colt reached the door and felt the wave of hatred in her words. He stopped and turned. *Here it comes.*

"I'm sorry, but I'm not into this. You're my mother's friend. Anyway, I was drunk last time."

92

The words had more force behind them than Colt intended. Fighting her and his own lust caused him to lose focus and become irritated.

Alison moved toward Colt. Her red face and zombie-like eyes reminded Colt of his dream.

"You can't do this to me. How would Mommy feel if I told her you got me drunk and then screwed me? How her sweet little boy took advantage of me?"

Colt was now on the defensive. This wasn't something he expected and he wondered if this was a real threat or not.

"Uh, um, why would you do that? You know it didn't happen that way."

"Maybe it did happen like that. I can remember what I want," screamed Alison.

"Goodbye. Leave me alone," yelled Colt.

Alison, who was now directly in front of Colt, slapped him. *Crap, I should have seen that coming.* The psychic pain was far more intense than the physical. He could feel the entire brunt of her emotional state. It felt like red and black thought clouds were assaulting him and spiked walls were closing in. *I have to get out; I have to get out.*

"That's right Colt, get the hell out of my sight! Run like a rat. But don't think you can get away with this," yelled Alison Monroe as she slammed the door behind him.

The next thing Colt remembered was driving down the road with a burning cheek and sweaty forehead. A menu of future possibilities bounced across his unsettled mind. None of the entrees were appetizing. *Crap, a whole lotta bad things can happen. I wonder how much she can screw up my life?*

Chapter 16

------Email-------
From: Strong, Amy[amystrong@aol.com]
To: Bower, Susan[sbower@hhs.edu]
Subject: I think he's cute

HI SUZY
I HEARD ABOUT THE FIGHT. I THINK COLT IS SO CUTE. I DON'T
CARE IF HES SHORT. HE HELPS PEOPLE. HIS SISTER TALKED TO
OUR SOCCER TEAM. WE ALL THINK SHES THE BEST. I WANT TO
GET TO KNOW COLT BETTER☺

AMY

------Email-------

Colt and Bobby had been working all afternoon fixing sick
computers. The school day had ended hours before, but they
were only now walking toward the parking lot to leave for home.
The young men felt a sense of satisfaction after helping many
teachers and administrators become productive again. A
computer virus had rampaged through Highline High's
computer network causing a variety of problems. The two
young men had been up to the task and all of the infected
devices were now working.

"Man, that virus was bad. I'm sure glad we had the right
updates to fix them," said Bobby.

"It's really great when it all goes right. I can remember lots of times when we were drowning in tricky problems and we had no idea what was wrong. Dude, we've learned some stuff."

As they walked around a corner toward the baseball fields below, they heard the rattling of a fence and someone yelling, "No, no."

Bobby could see that three teenagers had a much smaller boy surrounded. The frail-looking student was backed up against the fence. The bullies were pushing him from side to side and slapping him up and down his thin body. One of the assailants was yelling obscenities at the helpless victim. The boy had a look of utter terror on his dirty, reddened face.

Bobby had only been watching for a few seconds, but now saw someone running toward the group. At first he was so startled that he did not realize who it was. He turned to say something to his friend, but Colt was not there. Bobby looked back just in time to see Colt hurtle into the three attackers with arms swinging. His loud shrieks sounded like battle cries. Colt hit one of the three attackers shoulder high and knocked him off his feet. The other two were startled, but soon recovered.

The tallest one said "He's not that big, Andy. We can get him."

Colt kept swinging his arms as he moved around like a boxer. But now, the bullies had regained their composure and were closing in.

"You punks! Leave him alone." yelled Colt.

Colt looked at the victim and recognized him as a freshman that he had seen around campus. He motioned to him to get away. As he turned back to the fight, he felt his legs buckle as he was forced to the ground. The small mob of attackers held him down and pounded on him together from above. Colt kicked one attacker between his legs and felt things ease up a little, but

95

his head continued to take a beating. Just as Colt was starting to fade into darkness, he saw a large arm come between him and those cowering above.

One of his assailants was flung aside and slammed against the fence causing a high-pitched rattling sound. Next, one large, strong arm clamped around the last attacker's neck and he was thrown to the ground. As he hit the hard earth, air escaped from his chest with a whoosh.

Colt was free and stood up but found it difficult to stay balanced. For a moment, he felt like he would faint as the pain of his injuries came pounding in. *Uh oh, I better slow down a minute. I'm feeling a bit woozy.* After a few moments he regained his balance and managed to keep the pain at bay.

All three of the bullies were on the ground. One was curled up in a ball moaning and the other two were being held down in a choke hold by Bobby Jones. Both rough-looking teens had panic in their bulging eyes. Colt kicked each of them in the side.

"You want more, punks? You want more?" screamed Colt.

"No Colt, we didn't know it was you," whined one.

"Bobby, let'em go before I kill one of em." said Colt as he hit one of them on the side of the head.

"Just leave guys. Don't make me hurt you anymore. And don't mess with this little kid ever again," said Bobby.

The two de-fanged attackers got up and helped the boy who was curled up in pain. All of them were hurting, which brought a slight smile to Colt's face. They skulked away as fast as they could.

Bobby looked at Colt, who was sitting on a low wall now. His lower lip and nose were both bleeding, and his right eye was beginning to swell. In spite of his injuries, Colt was grinning.

"Hey, man, you should have waited for me. They pounded you pretty bad," said Bobby.

"Screw those guys. Hey, I just reacted. They pissed me off and all of a sudden I was going at them. Goddam punks! I hate guys like that."

"That kid was about to be really messed up. You saved his bacon," said Bobby.

"Well Bobinator, you saved me. Thanks Dude. I ended up taking the kid's place. Do you know his name?"

"I think it's Eddie Tate. I recognized him from the meeting at the Sweden's house."

"I'm glad we helped him, even if he is a freshman nerd. I hate guys that beat up weak kids," said Colt.

"Can you get home okay?"

"I can make it, but I know I'm going to be hurting soon. Really hurting."

"Later man," said Bobby when they reached the parking lot.

"I'll save you next time," said Colt.

Colt grimaced and slowly pulled himself up and out of the purple VW in front of his house. The pain was more noticeable now that the adrenaline had dissipated. *I must look like crap. I sure feel bad.* He walked through the front door and tried to scurry by the kitchen so that he wouldn't be seen. His condition slowed him down and it was obvious that he wasn't himself as he dragged past his unsuspecting mother at the kitchen sink. She looked up with bright eyes knowing that her son had come home. Her smile changed when she saw the condition that Colt was in. Blood was still running from his lower lip and nose. His swollen eye was starting to turn blue and purple. Leona's eyes glistened with tears at seeing her baby in pain.

"Oh no. Colt, what happened? Oh honey," cried Leona.

"I just had a little scuffle, Mom. I'll be okay."

"You get into the bathroom right now. I'm going to clean you up."

Colt moaned and angled toward the bathroom. He didn't feel like explaining what happened. He knew his mother would try to be brave, but that this would take an emotional toll on her.

Colt only said, "I helped a kid that was getting beat up, Mom."

Leona smiled behind the river of tears rolling down her cheeks.

"You always did hate bullies."

~~~

After being nursed and taking some aspirin, Colt hugged his mother and trudged to his bedroom. He opened his email to see if Bobby had sent any notes about the fight. There were 23 emails in the in-box. All of the notes were about the incident at the school. Bobby Jones sent a note with just a subject line, which said, "News travels fast."

One email was from Mr. Sweden, who thanked him for helping a fellow program member. Colt was surprised to see how fast word got around about an incident that had happened only a few hours before. Some of the notes were from people he had never met. One was from a girl named Amy Strong. *I remember Amy. She's in sports, I think.* When he saw her name, he forgot about his pain and felt a tingling sensation from head to toe. *There's something about that note. Why am I feeling like this?* Rather than reading it, he lay down on his bed and wondered what a pretty girl might write to a boy who just got beaten up. He only allowed himself to imagine that the note contained wonderful, interesting and surprising words. When his thoughts were wrapped in a pleasant package, Colt slipped into slumber. A peaceful smile illuminated his swollen face.

Chapter 17

------Email-------
From: Strong, Amy[AmyS@aol.com]
To: O'Brien, Colt[ColtOB@yahoo.com]
Subject: Hi Colt

HI COLT
    I THINK IT'S GREAT YOU HELPING THAT BOY. YOUR SISTER
TALKED TO OUR SOCCER TEAM. WE LIKE HER A LOT. I'M GOING
TO THE LAN PARTY. WILL YOU BE THERE?? MAYBE WE CAN TALK
OR SOMETHING. BYE

    AMY STRONG

------Email-------

Amy Strong sat staring at the computer screen. Long, light
brown hair was pulled back into a ponytail, making her round
face stand out. The fear in her bright blue eyes was in stark
contrast to her long, trim, athletic body. It was a body
strengthened from year-round soccer practice and games.

Moments before, after struggling for over an hour to find
the right words, she had clicked the icon that sent her note to
Colt O'Brien. During that time a stormy, emotional battle had
raged inside her young mind. Amy was so drawn to Colt O'Brien
after he came to the aid of a helpless boy that she had leapt out
of her comfort zone. Sending a note like this was not something
she had ever done or even thought about doing. Similar to
Bobby Jones, she had played it safe all of her life. She never got
into trouble and was pointed to as an example of what a good

99

girl should be. Colt represented much of what she had avoided all of her seventeen years of living. He was spontaneous, daring, and a little too into himself. He lived in a foreign land on the outskirts of the conventional sleepy little town where Amy resided. None of that mattered to her. She was on a bullet train that was racing toward something new, different and unknown. Beneath her fears a molten ball of excitement was growing. Amy felt more alive than ever before. Every commonsense argument that came into her mind was shot down by her desire to be with Colt. *You don't even know him. He probably has a girlfriend. You aren't pretty enough,* she thought. In the end, her inexplicable crush on someone she didn't know, except from a distance, prevailed. Now she would wait; wait to see if he would answer and what he would say. She would simmer in a twenty-question twilight zone, where the questions kept repeating over and over, and over again. Regret, frustration and doubts assaulted her. *What have I done? What have I done? Why do I want him so much?*

~~~

Colt was in his bedroom with phone in hand. He winced with each word that came out of his mouth.

"Hey Bobster, how are things?" he said.

"Hey man. Doin' okay. You called me. What's up?" answered Bobby.

"What the heck is a LAN party? The little geeks are having one. We're invited."

"Oh, Tommy Rice told me about that. It's a bunch of PC's connected together to play games. He said it was great. Count me in."

"How did I not know about this? It sounds like my kind of deal," said Colt.

"It's fairly new and before now not that many games worked on it. I know this is our kind of happening. This program might not be that bad after all. I can play games while you study your ass off. Works for me," said Bobby.

"Okay dude. I'll tell them that we'll show. Do you know Amy Strong? She sent me a note."

"Yeah, I know her. She's really nice. She was going out with some wimpy guy. I think she dumped him. I thought you were staying away from chicks?"

"I'm just asking. No big deal," said Colt.

"Sure Colt, anything you say. Whatever."

But, Colt was curious and felt a slight pull toward this mysterious girl. It was a deep undercurrent that seemed to be growing.

~~~

Sheets of rain bolstered by high winds, were coming down on the palatial Tate home. Waves, from the normally serene Puget Sound, hit the rock wall in front of the house with a force that created sprays of white, foamy mist. The large circular driveway in front of the large two-story house was crowded with wet vehicles of all makes and models. Young teenagers and adults dressed in raingear carried bulky boxes and bags into the house. After unloading the computer equipment, the vehicles were parked on a large lawn in the rear of the edifice.

Colt and Bobby stood in a huge basement recreation room. Computers and people were starting to stack up behind them as tables, cabling and other equipment were organized by Billy Carbon, Gunnar Sweden, and a few helpers.

"Hey Billy, what has to happen here to do the setup?" asked Colt.

Billy looked over at Colt with a bit of trepidation. Although he was very competent and up to the task, he was still a freshman and Colt a senior.

"Uh, hi Colt. Not that much, really. We need to have tables for the keyboards, mice and monitors. Then, we need stuff to plug into and hubs to cable the PCs together. Oh, and we need one machine to be a game server."

"Oh, is that all?" said Colt with a wry smile. "Can we help?"

"No need, we can do it. Probably the hard part will be getting all the different boxes to talk to one another. The software, I mean," said Billy.

Colt watched the younger boys build a system of networked computers. He could see that there would be at least twelve to fifteen machines connected. In spite of himself, he admired the knowledge, organization, and leadership that the young team demonstrated. *Crap, I better watch this. I've done two machines together, but not this many.* After about thirty minutes of physical setup and another forty minutes of fiddling with software, the local area network was up and running. It was time for the party to start.

Mr. Sweden walked up to front of the room. Behind him a white screen was rolling down from the ceiling. Every computer station had at least one teenage boy or girl sitting and one standing. More kids stood in other parts of the large room. Colt noticed that the party was open to more than the students who belonged to the certification program. He saw kids that he knew wouldn't have an interest in doing the required work. *I guess gaming can get a lot dudes and dudettes interested.*

Ron Sweden smiled and spoke.

"Welcome to our first LAN party. Before we start, I want to thank Mr. and Mrs. Tate for opening their home to us. I expect everyone to behave and have fun. Mr. Tate would like to say a few things.

102

A small balding man with glasses stood up in the back of the room.

"I just want to say that I think this is a wonderful program you guys have put together. Our son has really benefited from being a part of it. Also, I want to welcome Colt O'Brien to our home and thank him. He came to the aid of our son, Eddie, when he really was in a bad spot. Colt, are you here?"

Colt stood straight with chest out and grinned. He raised his hand and waved it from side to side.

"Right here, Mr. Tate. Thanks."

"No! Thank you, Colt. Eddie's mother and I are very grateful for what you did. We know you were injured, too," said Mr. Tate.

Colt, who was feeling heroic, felt a slight jab in his side. It irritated him until he looked into the eyes of Bobby.

"Oh, don't forget Bobby Jones. He was there, too," said Colt.

"Thanks to both of you, then," said Mr. Tate as he sat down.

"Pizza will be here soon, but until then we have chips and pop. Have a great time. You guys have earned it," said Ron Sweden.

The lights were dimmed as the large screen came alive with motion. A movie began. The hidden stereo system boomed out the sound track of the movie and smaller speakers emitted game sound effects. Colt played against ten other foes in a first-person shooter, action game. It took Colt a few minutes to get his bearings and understand the goal of the game. He found that points were earned by killing opponents using a vast array of different weapons which was nothing new to him. Eddie Tate sat next to Colt.

"Hey, Colt, you can send text after you kill a guy. You can rub it in. It's awesome," said Eddie.

103

"You know Eddie, I think I'm going to like this," said Colt.

After a warm-up period, the players all dove into the virtual gaming world. Screams of joyful victory and good-natured threats after defeat went across the room. Many players had on-going, on-line conversations with code names and specialized words to express their gamer personalities.

"You'll go down, Ogre."

"I'm the bringer of death."

"All punks will die."

"Here's some shrapnel to eat, dogs."

Colt loved functioning in this alternate world with weapons blasting and a wall of rock music surrounding him. He became engrossed in the game play and competition. Time was mutated in this LAN gaming world. It passed without notice as both Bobby and Colt became absorbed. After hours had been eaten up, something tugged at Colt's inner self. *Crap, that girl was supposed to be here. I forgot all about it and that's why I came.*

"Hey Bobierto, time for a break. You keep playing," said Colt.

"Okay Colt," said Bobby.

Colt decided to step outside into the blustery night. He still wondered about his reaction to Amy's email. He didn't want to have a girlfriend now, but her short note had affected him. He was almost obsessive in his curiosity about this young girl that he had never talked to. *Why can't I stop thinking about this? I don't even know her.*

The wind had died down and the rain was falling as a light mist. Some of the others, from the party, were on the patio facing the water. Colt felt Amy before he saw her. It was like a wave of nervousness hit him. *Well, if that's her, she's a little worried about something,* thought Colt. He saw her standing with another girl and sensed it was her that he was feeling. He noticed that she was a little taller than he had envisioned, which did not please him. He approached the two girls, who giggled a little. Amy fidgeted while looking down.

"Hi, uh you're Amy right? I'm Colt. Uh, I got your note. Sorry I didn't reply," said Colt.

She looked up into his eyes.

"Yes, I'm Amy. Oh, that's okay. It's great what you did for Eddie," said Amy.

"So, are you girls having a good time?"

"It's fun," said Amy.

Amy sent a knowing look to her friend, who turned and left. When they were alone Amy stared directly into Colt's eyes and smiled. When their eyes met Colt's world shook. His reaction was instant, overwhelming and like nothing he had ever experienced. Every part of him, body, mind and soul, was affected by her presence. He felt that an unseen force behind her eyes had filled him from head to toe. He thought of a golden sunset with distinct rays beaming into him from behind soft, billowy clouds, filling him with joy.

Whoa, this must be what love is. It has to be.

Amy was still talking, but Colt was trying to stop himself from hugging her. He didn't speak. After a time Amy started to cry, which snapped him back to the here and now.

"What's wrong?" asked Colt.

"I knew this was a bad idea. I never should have sent that note," sobbed Amy.

"Oh, no, don't think that. I just have a lot on my mind and I'm beat up. Let's go out for coffee or something."

"Do you really mean that? You're not just being nice?"

Colt felt like grabbing her and kissing her on the lips. He stopped himself by remembering that he was in a public situation with high school freshman. Also, he had no idea if she felt as strongly about him as he did about her. *This girl has affected me. I need to regroup before I do something stupid.*

"I mean it. I really mean it, Amy. Let's get together." said Colt.

When Amy realized that her desire to be with Colt was going to come true, she was overcome with happiness.

"Uh, okay. I better go now. I'm a mess." said the girl trying to avoid crying again.

Colt felt like Amy was a huge magnet and he was a tiny nail. It took all of his willpower to resist hugging her.

"I'll email you soon to set something up," said Colt.

Colt and Bobby were on their way home. The rain had stopped and the fresh, crisp air was filling Colt's senses.

"You aren't saying much," said Bobby.

"I think I'm back into chicks," said Colt.

Chapter 18

------Email-------
From: O'Brien, Colt[ColtOB@yahoo.com]
To: To: Jones, Bobby[Bobbyj@yahoo.com]
Subject: The heat is on

Hey Bobberino

Crap from all sides man. College this, college that. Or, can you take a test soon? When will they let up? They even have my sister hassling me.

Colt

------Email-------

Kelly O'Brien dialed home as was her usual custom on Saturday evenings after supper. Leona answered the phone.

"Hi Mom. How's everything?"

"Hi honey. I made sure that Colt was home when you called." answered Leona.

"Uhh, put him on, I guess," said Kelly.

"Hi Sis," said Colt.

"Hi Bro. How are things? Mom and Dad wanted me to give you some moral support."

Colts eyes looked up in frustration. His body tightened as his teeth clenched.

"Uh oh. What are we talking about? Is this more of the same old crap?"

"They're worried that you won't make it into college. Are you working at it? I thought you got Bs."

"I'm working hard, but it's a hassle. I got okay grades before but I sorta slowed down on that stuff. I just lost interest, I guess. Now, I'm trying to catch up. And, I'm trying to get a Microsoft certification."

"Let me know if I can help, but I don't know about computer stuff," said Kelly.

"Just love your brother like you always have, Sis," said Colt.

"I've been hearing that a certain soccer girl likes my little brother."

He hesitated. *Man, news travels fast. Geez, girls.*

"Oh, uh, you mean Amy? We're going to meet for coffee soon. We'll see what happens."

"I was impressed with her. So, it's really over with Staci?"

"The Staci thing is over. Let's not get in a hurry, though. I hardly know Amy. What's she like?"

"She's a great soccer player, a great student, and is really nice. I can't figure out why she would be interested in my little brother." said Kelly with a bit of sarcasm.

"I guess I'll find out for myself soon. When I met her, she seemed okay."

"Listen, Romeo, bear down on the schoolwork. We all want you to go to college next year. Put Mom back on so I can tell her I did the deed."

"Okay Kel. Pep talk is over. Later," said Colt.

"See ya," said Kelly.

~~~

Mr. Towne sat behind his desk and smiled at his visitors. The small man had a big, optimistic presence. Colt sat facing him between his mother and father. Both Leona and Robert smiled back at the friendly principal. Colt had the dazed look of a cornered animal with no energy to run.

"The good news is that Colt has done some work toward being accepted into college next year. With the help of our best counselor he's applied to three universities and is showing up more for class. As you know I like this young man and see great potential," said Mr. Towne.

Colt smiled as he glanced at his mother and leaned away from his father. He looked hopeful and a little confident.

"How about the bad news, Mr. Towne?" asked Robert.

"Colt's grades are borderline and we wonder if he can make the cut with grades alone. I'm looking at other options for him."

Robert O'Brien glared and his son while Colt looked for a place to duck as he fidgeted in his chair. Leona, in turn, shot angry darts at her husband, who leaned back with arms crossed.

"It sounds like there's still hope. What can Colt do to better his chances?" asked Leona.

Robert leaned forward ready to speak and his tiny wife's arm shot across Colt and landed on her husband's chest. Robert closed his mouth. Mr. Towne smiled with his hands together.

"I think we have a possible way for Colt to be accepted. I've been brainstorming with Colt's counselor and Mr. Sweden, who is running the certification program."

Hope was reflected in Leona's eyes. She spoke.

"Is there a way to get him in?" she asked.

"Most universities need computer technical support. Also, it appears that the certification Colt is trying to achieve is highly regarded at all of the schools we care about."

"I thought this computer stuff was a waste of time," said Robert.

"Not anymore. Too many of us rely on computers to get work done. School computers hold student records, grades, and other very important information now. Also, it's anticipated that the Microsoft certifications will be accepted for college credit soon," said Mr. Towne.

The energetic principal continued.

"Colt needs to keep his grades up, continue helping out with computers and, most of all, pass the certification exam. Then, we'll have a great success story to tell my contacts in higher education. I feel confident that he'll be accepted if he does those things."

"This is wonderful. Oh, Colt, I'm so happy," said Leona.

"How is he supposed to pass this test if he never studies?" moaned Robert.

"I encourage all of you to work together to support him. Mr. Sweden, Mr. Carbon, and their group will help also," said Mr. Towne with a confident smile.

Colt said nothing. *Dude, you thought it was all so easy. Now you know it's not.* He was finding that doing school work was simple compared to the certification material he was attempting to learn. *Crap, I study and study, but I can't even pass the stupid practice test. How am I ever going to get through this? And now he says I don't go to college unless I pass it.* Colt looked at Mr. Towne who seemed very confident that a little study and perseverance would pull Colt through. *Oh right, Mr. Towne. All I have to do is pass the easy little certification test. Well maybe it isn't that easy.*

Robert looked at Mr. Towne while leaning on Colt a little more than usual. Colt tried to resist so he wouldn't push on his mother.

"Well, he's gotten himself into this fix. Let's see if he can get out."

"Robert, let's try to be supportive. Mr. Towne thinks Colt will be fine," said Leona.

"If he can do this, then I'll take back what I've been saying. That's a big if, though."

On the drive home, Colt's thoughts turned to the other big issue in his life. Amy Strong had captured his heart. Colt somehow knew that he was destined to be with her. *How can that be? We only talked for a few minutes.* When she appeared in his mind, which was often, he lost the sense of being a single person. It was as if they were connected from long ago. This inner sense of union scared and thrilled him at the same time. He felt like a strong tide was pulling him toward the horizon and he was helpless to affect it. *What's happening to me? Whoa Dude. Hang on.*

Chapter 19

------Email-------
From: Strong, Amy[AmyS@aol.com]
To: Bower, Suzy[sbower@hhs.edu]
Subject: It's not really a date

HI SUZY

I'M MEETING COLT AT STARBUCKS. I HOPE HE DOESN'T THINK I'M
DORKY. I WONDER IF I LIKE HIM TOO MUCH. WHAT DOES IT MEAN
IF I THINK ABOUT HIM AT LEAST ONCE EVERY TEN MINUTES?
THIS IS SURE DIFFERENT☹

AMY

------Email-------

Amy Strong had been on the phone with her friend, Suzy
Bower, for hours. She didn't have a cell phone and was happy
that no one was at home to interrupt her. This was a time when
having phone privacy was crucial. Her date with Colt was only
about an hour away.

"I'm going to wear the tight jeans and my soccer sweatshirt.
What do you think?" said Amy.

Suzy was silent for a few moments, which was not like her.

"Hmmm. That sounds so boring. You know he's a flashy
dresser. Wear your green blouse. It looks great on you," said
Suzy.

"This isn't even a date. It's just coffee. We're only going to
talk a little."

"Oh, is that so? You could have fooled me. You've only been nerved out all day. Do you think you're talking to your mom or something? Jeez."

"Okay, so I'm a little nervous and maybe excited. Wouldn't you be?" said Amy.

"I don't know what I'd be. Wear some makeup. You don't put enough on."

Amy was now becoming frustrated. She wanted support without the advice.

"You know I hate wearing makeup. I wasn't wearing any last time I saw him."

"Amy, you can really look cute if you make a little effort. I wish I had that athletic body like you have. You have it made."

"Ok, I'll do what you say. I think the purple tennis shoes will be good, too," said Amy.

"Are you sure you want to do this? You know he has a reputation of being into numero uno. Staci Parks is really sad that he dumped her. You could get hurt."

"I've heard that stuff, but I don't think he's really like that. Anyway, I'm getting sick of being nice and cautious all the time. Nothing ever happens."

"Yeah, I know the feeling, Amy. I know the feeling."

~~~

It was rainy and cold outside Colt's window. He stared out at the gray, stormy day, but his focus was inward. *Why am I so nervous? It's just a girl.* For hours he'd been recounting recent events, trying to see what happened to make him feel so out of sorts. After finally getting to the point where he thought he was in control as far as girls were concerned, now he felt like a bowl of emotional mush. The freedom he felt from not having a girlfriend, and telling Alison Monroe to leave him alone had disappeared. He sensed that he was about to be trapped. He knew that he was about to step into the cage, but could not conjure up the energy to be concerned. He was beginning to feel like it was inevitable. *Man, I'm swinging all over the place. I think I'm too tired to be confident.* On one end of the spectrum he was acting logical and responsibly. He studied for the certifications and was generally doing the right things to please his parents. On the other, messier end, he was bouncing from one emotional state to another. In his mind were vivid images of an aggressive, lusty Ali Monroe, his recent fight and now his inexplicable infatuation with a girl he didn't know. *How did I end up falling for her? I can't even think about her without breaking into a sweat. What is it about her that is pulling at me?*

Colt's thoughts were interrupted by the ringing phone.

"Colt here. What up?"

"Hey Colt, aren't you gone yet? Where are you going again?" said Bobby.

Colt was irritated that his train of thought was hi-jacked.

"Starbucks. I'm meeting her at Starbucks."

"Oh yeah. Gonna get some java. Say hi for me."

"Dude, what is this call for? I'm already getting a little tense with this deal. I'm starting to wonder why I'm even doing it. Are you trying to piss me off or what?"

"Hey man, lighten up. We're buds, remember? I'm here to support you in your entry back into the chick world," said Bobby.

"Get lost. We're just going to talk," said Colt.

"You keep telling yourself that, my friend."

Colt could hear the teasing smile in his friend's voice.

"Lay off, dude. Later."

As Colt hung up he decided that he'd had enough of doubts and mental gymnastics. *Dude, just show up to this thing and see what happens.*

~~~

Colt walked rapidly toward the Burien Starbucks in the pouring rain. He was wearing a muted red parka with the hood up. He opened the door and was assaulted by a pungent aroma of roasted coffee, bright lights and warm air. Amy was sitting alone in a corner with a cup of coffee. She was nervous but radiant in her bright green blouse and light dusting of makeup. As Colt approached, he inhaled her delicate but penetrating perfume and noticed that she was wearing a light shade of lipstick.

The sense of cool that he wanted to maintain left him like birds taking flight. His desired aloofness was replaced with an instant intoxication. All parts of him were becoming open and receptive. Everything was brighter, softer and friendlier. Colt was aroused sexually, emotionally and intuitively.

He smiled and sat. "Hi Amy."

"Hi. I got here early, so I ordered. I usually like just coffee without the other stuff," said Amy.

"I'll go and get just coffee, too. I'll be right back."

Colt waited in line trying to get his bearings. He knew this was not like him, but he was enjoying this drug-like state so much that he could not let it go. *This feels great. It's like a flood of everything good.* He saw vivid movie-like pictures moving across his inner view. Amy was a glowing princess and he was a prince. They were enjoying each other's compnay while doing fun and exciting activities. His sense of contentment deepened. He

115

somehow ordered and paid for his coffee. As he sat down, he noticed that Amy was agitated about something.

Still, Colt felt at ease and his eyes reflected an inner happiness.

"Is something wrong?" he asked.

"Oh, I don't know. I wonder if I should be here. I hardly know you."

"It's okay. You know my sister. And, soon you'll know me better. You might not know this, but I was really into soccer, too."

In spite of her nervousness, Amy relaxed at the mention of her favorite activity. This was an area where she had experienced great success and joy. Doubts were overcome by curiosity and increasing confidence.

"Really? You were? When?"

"I played until the end of junior high. Then I got interested in computers."

"I love everything about soccer," she said.

Now that she felt more comfortable, Amy began to talk more. The words flowed out of her with increasing openness. Colt's intoxication grew with each minute he was with her. She seemed so genuine and beautiful. The beauty that he recognized was inside and outside. Colt forgot that relationships tied him down. He forgot to hide his feelings. He forgot that he wasn't supposed to fall in love. Most of all, he forgot about all of the vexing items on his internal list. Colt relaxed and through being together a bond formed between them.

"Listen Amy, I think we did okay for a cup of coffee meeting, don't you?"

"I really liked it, Colt," said Amy.

"Why don't we go to a movie or something?"

"Really? Uh, er, um sure," said Amy.

"Great. I'll call you to set something up," said Colt.

The two teenagers walked toward Amy's car. The rain had stopped and a sliver of sunlight was slicing through gray clouds. When they got to her car Amy turned toward Colt.

There seemed to be a natural force pulling them toward each other.

Colt said, "I really had a great time, Amy."

With a lunge, Amy grabbed and hugged Colt tight. She hoped that he didn't see the tears of joy gushing down her cheeks and streaking her makeup. Colt smiled while floating on a sea of serenity.

Chapter 20

------Email-------
From: Gray, Jennifer[jenniferG@microsoft.com]
To: Sweden, Ron[swedenr@yahoo.com]
Subject: Your visit to Microsoft

Hello Ron

It was great talking to you about a field trip to the Microsoft campus. We are very excited about having your group visit. I will be showing you around. As we discussed, I have arranged specific activities for your students. After hearing about what you've accomplished and your enthusiasm about Microsoft and our products, we expect this to be a great experience for your group and for us.

I did ask if Mr. Gates would be able to meet with you. Unfortunately, that will not be possible.

Maps, directions and itinerary are enclosed. Please call me with any questions.

Regards
Jennifer

------Email-------

The Highline High campus was empty. Colt drove his VW bug into the circular driveway at the rear of the school, parked and jumped out. He was wearing a white shirt and tie beneath a bright purple jacket with slacks. He hopped up and down for a few minutes. *I need to relax. I'm way too jacked up.* The sing-song ring of his cell phone pealed through the brisk, dry air.

"Hey dude," said Colt.

"What the hell, I should be going to this deal," said Bobby.

Colt smirked at knowing how much his friend wanted to go on this field trip.

"Crack a book and pass a test. Maybe you can go on the next one," said Colt.

"You haven't even passed a test yet. Crap, I need to be going, too."

"I'll call you after and tell you how it went. Do you think we'll see Bill Gates?

"Screw you, Colt. Damn it. You could have gotten me into this thing."

"I tried Bobinator. No luck, amigo. Sorry. Gotta go."

"I still can't believe you're leaving me behind."

"See ya," said Colt.

Other vehicles were now arriving. Ron Sweden, who was the first one there, beamed when Mr. Towne approached him. He was very proud that the school principal was coming along. To him, this gave credence to what they were doing. Soon about 15 students and four adults were gathered in front of Mr. Carbon and Mr. Sweden. Mr. Sweden addressed the assembled group.

"We'll be using the three mini-vans for transportation. Mr. Towne and I will go in my car and lead the way. Are we all set?"

Colt wrestled with his tie, which made him look like he was hanging himself.

"Why did we have to wear the ties?" he asked a bit irritated.

"You're representing Highline High School. For today, it's the rule. With that purple jacket on, you'll be hard to miss anyway. " said Mr. Carbon.

After a 25-minute drive, the caravan exited the freeway in Redmond. Billy leaned over to Gunnar.

"I bet we're late. It's easy to get lost on the side streets."

"I hope not. How would that look? They do this big deal for us and we can't even make it on time."

After driving in circles for about thirty minutes, the caravan finally turned into the Microsoft campus and parked next to a white, one-story building. The diminutive Mr. Towne shot out of the lead car with nervous eyes darting everywhere. The rest of the group seemed unaffected by their late arrival. The bright sun, shining through the crisp winter air, gave them a sense of gleeful anticipation.

A tall, slender, dark-haired woman stood on the steps leading to the front door. She appeared to be in her late 20s and wore blue jeans with a long-sleeved, light, blue shirt. The word "Microsoft" was sewn on the front. *Here we are in ties and she's dressed casual,* thought Colt. *Not bad looking, too.*

"Hi, I'm Jennifer Gray. Let's get everybody checked in. Then we can start." said the young woman in a direct, confident way.

The group followed Jennifer to a desk where they were given badges. After, they formed a circle around the Microsoft representative. She re-introduced herself and gave a short welcome speech. She smiled at the young students and pointed toward the door.

"Let's get into the mini-bus. Our first stop will be the data center. We'll be there in a few minutes." she said.

Colt had few expectations about what a data center was like. Now he was becoming curious. When they walked in, Jennifer stopped at an area that had about fifty computer screens. *Wow! A wall made up of monitors,* thought Colt.

"This is the control center. Systems are watched here twenty-four hours a day," said Jennifer.

"Is this the data center?" asked Gunnar.

"The data center is monitored from here, but this is not it."

"So, what is the data center for?"

"All of our server-based software is tested in the data center before we release it. Also, we have lots of applications like Email, file sharing, and databases running on the servers. Let's go in."

The group passed through nondescript double doors into the computer area. Before Colt could get a good view, he was pummeled by psychic waves of kinetic energy. He sensed electrical particles moving everywhere within the sterile smelling enclosure. Once he was able to see the contents of the room, he was struck by the enormity. Before him was a series of giant, enclosed, air-conditioned rooms. There were no windows. It was almost cold with a slight steady movement of dry air. A never-ending, dull droning hum surrounded the visitors. As the group walked down rows of connected racks filled with computers and related equipment Colt gasped. He could see that a tile in the floor was pulled up, revealing hundreds of cables beneath. Green and amber lights blinked randomly from the thousands of devices in the room. Colt turned to Mr. Carbon, who seemed to be at home in this environment.

"This is huge. I can't believe how much stuff is in here."

"I heard that they have another data center just as big," said Matthew.

"Where is everybody?" asked Colt.

"This is what's called a lights-out operation. Most of the work is done remotely. They can even configure and load the computers from outside."

As they walked through the enormous computer facility, Colt felt like he was in the center of the computing universe. He tried to comprehend the multiple connections, processing power, and cost of the equipment he was viewing. With his inner vision he saw millions of connections threaded together in a

121

universal blanket. He was in awe of the sheer size of it all and could not fathom how much of an impact this one data center had. His past experience with fixing individual computers seemed miniscule compared to all of these networked computers working together. As the small group exited the data center, Colt allowed the experience to soak in. *Man, do I have a lot to learn. It goes on forever.*

The next stop on the tour was a session with more Microsoft representatives. As the students followed Jennifer they passed a break room. A wide-eyed Billy turned to Colt.

"See all that pop and coffee in the room? Anybody that works here gets as much as they want for free." he said.

"Nice perk. I have a feeling this is a great place to work," said Colt.

The group assembled in a comfortable meeting room with seating, tables, white board and projector. A diminutive woman in her mid-thirties was the first to speak. She had short brown hair, sparkling bright blue eyes, and a direct personality. Her area of expertise was recruiting new employees. She talked about the values of her company and the characteristics that Microsoft looked for in an employee. *This lady sure walks the talk. I can see why they hired her,* thought Colt. After about ten minutes of talking, she asked if there were questions.

Billy spoke first.

"What is the most important thing you look for?"

"Many who apply to work with us are smart and hard working. However, the thing we look for most is the passion to make the world a better place. The key is to use that passion to make great products. We create an environment for that to happen and try to fill it with talented, enthusiastic individuals.

"What about education?" asked Eddie Tate.

"Education is the foundation of any career. You won't get very far without at least a bachelor's degree. Many of our employees also have advanced degrees."

The next person to speak was the head of internships. He discussed the program and opportunities that were available to high school and college students. At the end of his talk, he seemed somewhat embarrassed.

"I tried taking one of the exams that many of you have already passed. I'm sorry to say that I didn't pass. Those questions are really difficult. Everybody here is impressed with the great things that you all have accomplished."

Yeah, well not all of us have passed the cert test yet, thought Colt. He felt like he had awakened from a long nap and everything had changed. *Man, this is for real. If I want to play, I guess I better do the education thing. Hell, that's just the entry fee in this place. Being smart isn't enough. You have to prove it.* He regretted that he hadn't earned a certification yet. He looked at the younger students and cringed. *The little nerds are passing me up. I can't let that happen.*

As the group approached the last stop of their visit, most of the students became excited and talkative. Eddie Tate looked at Colt with an enthusiastic smile.

"We're going to the store. This is awesome," he said.

The Microsoft store was famous in Western Washington. The store sold Microsoft software along with apparel and other items. Employees received a large discount on merchandise. Every teenage computer geek wanted to visit the store with an employee. The Highline group was given the discounted prices as part of their visit. *I better not forget Bobby. It was bad enough that he couldn't come along. Let's see what they have.* Colt looked at the clothes and decided to buy a light gray jacket and baseball style cap. He was surprised at how little the items cost and decided to purchase the Windows NT operating system for his home computer also. At the register Colt saw Ron Sweden talking with someone. He turned to Gunnar who was in line next to him.

"Gunnar, who is that talking to your dad? He looks important."

"That's a guy from the Microsoft paper. It's an interview about the program. It should be out next month."

"They have a newspaper?"

"Yeah, it's for the employees, I guess. We get interviewed all the time. My dad says that we're putting Highline School District on the map."

As the kids and parents walked down the stairs from the Microsoft store with shopping bags in hand, the line in front of Colt stopped. He bumped into Eddie Tate, almost knocking him down the stairs. Colt sensed a referential, almost spiritual aura around the group. As he looked down over the railing, he understood why. Bill Gates was strolling through the front door with two individuals who seemed to be assistants. Not only had his group stopped in its tracks, but everyone near Mr. Gates was also motionless. Colt watched the computing superstar with laser focus. He could not believe that he was seeing the most famous individual in the computer world. Then something happened that stunned the rapt young students hovering in anticipation on the stairs. Bill Gates stopped, looked up at the group, smiled and winked. He then continued into the building. Colt felt the referential fog being blown away by joyful sparks arcing between the young students. It was a psychic fireworks display that only Colt could see.

Billy and Gunnar together uttered the word, "Whoaaaaaaaaa."

On the ride home, Colt did not say anything. He was absorbing everything that he had experienced at Microsoft. Seeing Bill Gates in person made everything more real to him.

He was now inspired to strive to achieve more than he had ever considered. He saw a window of opportunity in front of him. He knew that the window was open now, but would soon close. Certain realities that his cockiness had allowed him to ignore were becoming crystal clear to him. He could see that without an education his options would be dismal. Also, if he wanted to be recognized as a proficient computer technician, he needed to prove it by obtaining the certification.

I can't believe that the little geeks are the key to my future. But, it's gotta be true. And it's time for me to get totally on board.

Chapter 21

------Email-------
From: Sweden, Gunnar[gunman@yahoo.com]
To: Carbon, Billy[billg@hocs.biz]
Subject: We savd him
----

billg

we savd him. he had no clue. I can't believe it he was sooooo surprisd.

gunman

------Email-------

Robert faced Colt from behind a large desk in his den. *What the hell? Only bad things happen here. At least he doesn't look pissed off. What can he want now?* Father and son rarely talked. Colt felt invisible to his father unless he did something to upset him, which seemed to be the norm. *I don't need him to get mushy on me, but it might be nice for him to notice me once in a while,* thought Colt as he kept guessing what the reason was for this meeting. The college thing, that Robert had been pushing lately, was more for the status of the O'Brien name than his welfare. At least that was how Colt felt. It was difficult for him to read his father, but he usually could tell if he was mad about something. Now, Robert seemed even-tempered rather than smoldering. The psychic buzz that Colt could sometimes sense was absent. *I think my dad is a buzz-free zone. Everything is hidden. He always has the upper hand.* Colt braced himself for whatever might come from his intimidating father.

"Colt, I've been asking around about this new computer thing. I still have my doubts, but it seems that it's a viable part of most businesses. I'm told by my colleagues that it will continue to become more important."

Colt cheered up, hoping that this might get his father to stop riding him. *Maybe he can see that I'm doing something cool.*

"Yeah, I think it's really a big deal. That's why I'm going for the certification."

"We both know that you've been slacking for awhile. You'll need to have a change in attitude to earn that certification. You still need to keep your grades up, too."

"I'll make it. I'm studying a lot. I really want to get into college."

"I wanted to talk because I have a job for you. A friend of mine has computers and he's having a problem. He needs help and will pay. I told him you could help."

"Sure, I can take a look. What's the problem?"

"He only said it had something to do with Exchange Server. I have no idea what that is. I'll give you his number."

"Okay Dad. I'm happy to help. I'll fix whatever the problem is."

"If you can do this, it will make me look good. So, do a good job."

"No problem," said Colt.

What the hell is Exchange Server? Sure Colt, you can do anything. Maybe you should learn to spell it before you volunteer. Ahhhhhh!

~~~

The Netscape browser results stared back at Colt. He had typed in *Exchange* and 300,522 hits came back. Most of the links on the page referred to email or server. It required extreme self-control for Colt to focus on this new problem in his life and not to look for other less tiresome topics on the Internet. He clicked on a link that listed *Microsoft Exchange Server* and was transferred to the Microsoft web site. He was relieved to see that Exchange was a Microsoft product, but his intuitive feeling was that of being under water in a fast-moving current. He thought that a server was a bigger version of a workstation, but that was about it. After reading, it was obvious that Exchange was an email system that needed Windows NT Server to work. *Crap, I'm not that far yet. I'm just studying for the Workstation test.* He read further and wondered if he could fix any problem related to this new thing he was seeing. *I sure don't need the old man to see me screw this up. And the freshmen geeks will think I'm an idiot. I'll buy a book, study up, and fix this problem. It can't be that hard.*

Colt had picked up a book and scanned it to see what he was up against. He understood some of the subject matter, but was not soaking in the information like he wanted to. After selecting a few chapters and reading them like his life depended on understanding what was in them, he stopped in frustration. *I told the old man that I could do this but now I wonder. Crap, this is not easy stuff.* Colt decided to see if he could recruit some backup support. He called Mr. Carbon in desperation.

"Hi, Mr. Carbon, this is Colt O'Brien."

"Oh, hi Colt. How is the studying going?"

"It's going good. I was wondering if any of you guys know about Exchange Server?"

"Billy and Gunnar are pretty good at anything server related. What's up?"

"Well, I have a job to fix a problem, but I don't know much about it."

"How about this? You see how far you get. If you need help, call Billy or Gunnar. I'll let them know what you're doing."

"Thanks Mr. Carbon."

"Remember, you can't always do it alone. Sometimes another set of eyes can really help."

Matthew Carbon looked up at his son Billy.

"That was Colt. He may need some help with an Exchange problem."

"Why can't Flash fix it himself? He acts like he knows everything," said Billy.

Matthew aimed a fierce stare at his son.

"You know what we're about. We help each other. Don't hurt yourself by getting into that crap. You and Gunnar are the best in the program, but if you don't help the other students you're only halfway there."

"Okay Dad. I guess I forgot that part," said Billy sheepishly.

~~~

Colt had been working on the Exchange Server problem for long enough to know that he was in way over his head. After arriving, he had been informed that the company tech support person had been trying to fix the problem for over a week. He also was told that there were two email servers and not one. He was able to log on and restart both servers, but both of them had screens of error messages when starting. After they did finally seem to be working, email was not being sent. Colt didn't know what was wrong and he didn't have the right utilities to look at the problem. Colt made the call.

"Hello," said Billy Carbon.

"Hi, Billy. I'm having a problem with some Exchange servers. I thought you guys might want to take a look."

"Sure, man. My dad said you were working on a server problem. Gunnar and I can come over. Just tell me where it is."

"Thanks Billy."

Ron Sweden pulled into the parking lot with Gunnar and Billy. Because they were not old enough to drive, parents needed to give them rides when opportunities like this one came up. Ron walked behind the young boys who were carrying bags filled with software and computer tools. Colt met them at the door.

"Follow me. I'll tell you guys what's happening."

Both Billy and the taller Gunnar walked with a casual seriousness. The young boys were confident and at a young age, already looked like professionals. No one who saw them would doubt that they were there to work. After Colt told them the little that he knew, Gunnar asked one question.

"Do they have internet access here?"

"I'll ask the lead guy," Colt replied.

Gunnar turned to Billy.

"You take that box and I'll take this one."

"Sounds good to me, but I think I know what it is already," said Billy.

"Yeah, it's about five versions of hot fixes behind, right?" said Gunnar.

"That's my guess," said Billy.

Colt returned looking agitated and hopeful.

"Yeah, they have the internet. You can get to it from any of their computers."

Gunnar spoke to Colt with more confidence that ever before.

"We're going to download hot fixes and install them. It shouldn't take too long. Hot fixes are software updates that fix problems. Once we have that done, we'll see how things look."

The two boys worked without speaking except to verify that they had found the correct software on the Microsoft web site. After about forty minutes the young techies turned to each other, gave the thumbs up sign, and hit the power button on the two Exchange servers.

Five minutes later they could hear someone yell from a desk in another room, "I've got email, a lot of email."

Gunnar and Billy slapped hands in a high five and smiled. Ron Sweden watched from a distance. He grinned and clapped his hands, but made no noise.

Ron approached the three teenagers.

"Now, that's teamwork. You guys worked together and got the job done." he said with a broad grin.

Colt started to say that he hadn't done anything, but instead said, "I think I like working as a team."

Chapter 22

------Email-------
From: O'Brien, Colt[ColtOB@yahoo.com]
To: Jones, Bobby[Bobbyj@yahoo.com]
Subject: No rest for Colt

Hey Boppinbobbin

I have never studied so much in my life. Crap - this is like pulling teeth with pliers. I can see that I get serious or crash and burn.
At least my regular school work is easy now.

Colt

------Email-------

After weeks of studying, Colt's frustration level was high. His plan of attack was being carried out with tenacity, but he was not seeing the results that he wanted. *Why am I not getting this NT crap? If the little nerds can do it, why is it so hard for me?* He tried to put his emotions in check so that he could understand how to improve his study regimen. He inhaled deep breaths for about five minutes with eyes closed. This allowed him to analyze his situation.

I'm working hard enough, but am I working smart enough? He cringed when remembering being saved from humiliation by Billy and Gunnar. He smiled when recalling being in awe at Microsoft, but then thought of Gunnar and Billy, who seemed right at home. It was like they were born on the Microsoft campus. The hours of reading, the practice tests; it was more work than he had ever dreamed he could do. It seemed like that much effort should have more of a return. *Maybe I should bail out? No way. Screw that idea. No stupid test can break me. I can do this.*

As he was analyzing the situation he sensed something and his mind formed a picture. It was a clear view of painted clouds with a light blue background. Colt felt an immediate serenity. He had recognized a specific feeling first and then the mental image followed. As he viewed what he thought to be the clouds on the ceiling of the purple house, he felt a presence. It reminded him of his mother, but seemed to be more ethereal. *I wonder what that is? Hmmm? Maybe I should make a call.*

"Hello."

"Er, uh, uh, hi. I'm trying to get a hold of Mr. Carbon. This is Colt O'Brien. Is this the right number?"

"Oh yes, Colt. I'm Mr. Carbon's wife, Elyce. I thought you might call."

That voice. It goes right through me. Weird, thought Colt.

"Oh, uh, you thought I was going to call? Why's that?" asked Colt.

"I just had a feeling. Sometimes that happens to me." Elyce replied.

"You know, I get feelings sometimes, too," said Colt hoping that she would talk more.

"Nice talking with you, Colt. Good luck with your computer thing. Here's Matthew."

Man, that was short. Crap, I had more questions.

"This is Matthew."

"Uh, hi, Mr. Carbon. I'm reading and doing practice tests, but it's like I'm going backwards," said Colt.

"You're not alone. If this was easy everybody would be doing it."

133

Colt was a bit surprised that he seemed to be in the majority after having his confidence shaken.

"You mean it's this hard for everybody?"

"Like any new thing, when you first start out, it takes time to get your bearings and move forward." answered Matthew.

"I'm wondering if I'm doing something wrong."

"I have a saying. Repetition is your friend. Our approach is to use all the different resources available to us and to keep studying until we know it."

"Well, I'm reading and doing practice tests."

"Here are the steps. Read more than one book until you understand it. Do practice tests and read the answers to the questions you miss. Try out what you're learning on an NT Workstation. If you keep doing all of that over and over, you'll eventually learn it."

"Well, I haven't installed NT yet, but I've been doing the other stuff," said Colt.

"You need to do that. Start using NT on your home machine. It will help. Also, remember that passing the exam is not the same as fixing a computer problem. Many of the questions are not realistic situations. They'll ask you things that you'll never see in a work situation."

"Those practice questions are so long. I get a headache just reading them."

"If you keep at it, eventually they'll make sense. I also have been giving classes on some of the material, but I don't think you've been to any yet. How about this? Billy and I will meet with you and go over what you're doing. I'll bring my class materials and answer any of your questions. Okay?"

"You'd do that?" asked Colt.

"Give me a time and place," said Matthew.

"What about now?"

"Billy isn't here now, but I can go over the materials with you. Shoot by."

The meeting had been exactly what Colt needed. Mr. Carbon was thorough and organized. He went over the outlines he used for his lectures and talked about tricky topics. He also suggested techniques to approach areas of study. After Mr. Carbon was finished, Colt asked questions. He was surprised and pleased that the fog blocking his learning was starting to dissipate. Most important was that he now felt confident that he had a good approach.

"This has been great, Mr. Carbon. I really feel like I'm getting it," said Colt.

"I could tell from your questions that you know a lot of the material. It just takes that extra step of connecting the dots. I'm glad this helped," said Matthew.

"The part about the difference between share permissions and file permissions really makes sense now. Thanks."

"Just pass the exam. And don't forget, when you think you're ready we'll do an assessment. No one has ever failed if they pass the assessment."

"Okay, thanks again."

"It does get easier, Colt. Keep working. Take it easy. I'll see you later."

Man, this guy has it down. He knows this crap. It's like he uncovered the hidden stuff.

As Colt walked by the picture window on the front porch of the Carbon home, he saw a diminutive woman with dark red hair. He felt her presence as much as saw her. She looked at him and nodded as he walked away. *That's what I was feeling before. She's somehow connected with that odd feeling I had.*

~~~

The computer displayed a screen with a logon box and waited for input. One line was for user name and one was for password. Colt knew from his study that this was a requirement for Windows NT. There was no way to access the functions of the computer without logging in. Colt was pleased that he had installed the new operating system with few problems. It was not difficult after he decided to follow the steps listed in one of the NT books. *Now, I can have hands-on experience and not just books. This should really help me connect the dots.*

Colt answered the ringing phone.

"Hello."

"Hey man, what are you doing?" said Bobby.

"I just installed NT. Now I can dig into this. I'm sick of just reading about it. I went over to the Carbons and got educated."

"What happened over there? The last time you were just mellow."

"For one thing I saw what his wife looks like. And I talked to her on the phone. I could tell she decorated that living room. She has a vibe."

"Wow, I think that would be interesting. I mean, meeting the person who paints clouds on the ceiling," said Bobby.

"Anyway, Mr. Carbon explained a lot of stuff. I guess I was so into learning from him that I forgot to get too laid back. I think I can almost pass the test now. Also, he said that I needed to use NT," said Colt.

"What about device drivers? Have you had any problems with that?"

"I haven't gotten that far yet. Come over if you want. We can break it together," said Colt.

"I can't believe you put that on your PC. Half of your stuff probably won't work now. We both know how bad it can be even if you're just upgrading Windows."

"I had to commit to this and deal with whatever happens. I've got a lot of reasons to get this certification now. Besides, I hear that most of the stuff runs on it."

"I'll cruise over. Maybe I can learn something, too," said Colt's friend.

Chapter 23

------Email-------
From: Bower, Suzy[sbower@hhs.edu]
To: Strong, Amy[AmyS@aol.com]
Subject: What's the latest

HI Amy

So..... what is going on with the new flame? We have to meet so you can tell me all the juicy details. I hope you don't get hurt. It's so obvious that you've fallen for Colt.

Your Friend SusyQ

------Email-------

Pockets of water were forming in the indentations on the track that encompassed the multi-purpose field at Highline High. A steady rain pelted the teenage girls running across the field after a black and white soccer ball. Both teams of elite players were drenched, but didn't seem discouraged. A small crowd cheered under umbrellas and makeshift coverings. Amy Strong ran past mid-field moving swiftly along the sideline. The slim, athletic, young woman ran smooth, fast and in complete control of her body. In a game with many talented players, she stood out as exceptional, as her long strides distanced her from competitors. Amy's confidence and skills were evident.

One of Amy's teammates paused while controlling the ball at the center of the sloppy field while looking for an opening.

With a rush, an opposing player attacked splashing water in all directions. Both girls kicked and by chance, the wet ball sailed away from them toward the goal. Amy made a sharp cut and slashed into the center of the field to reach the slow-moving globe. She arrived just before two opposing players and took control. Amy leaned, twisted, kicked, dribbled and outran three opponents in her ferocious march toward the goal. Now, only one defender remained between her and the wide-eyed goalie who was slightly crouched anticipating a shot on goal. As the quick, determined defender charged at her, Amy surveyed the situation for a moment and calculated her next move. When her opponent came upon her, running fast, Amy stopped, turned completely around, and leaned just enough to make contact with the opposing player, but not to cause a foul. The smaller girl flew sideways and away from Amy, who now had a sparkling, competitive gleam in her eyes. She turned and sprinted toward the tense goalie in front of the net. When ten yards away from the goal, she kicked the ball with such force that the goalie could only see a flash of black and white slamming into the other side of the net. The shrill sound of the whistle filled the air. Fans cheered as teammates crowded around Amy. The referee blew again and yelled, "Halftime."

Amy walked toward the sidelines. Her friend Susy, who was covered in rain gear, was looking at Amy and making hand gestures toward the end of the group of fans. Amy looked in the indicated direction, saw a flash of bright day-glo red, and knew who was there. A sense of confusion and weakness replaced her confidence and joy. *Oh no, why is he here? Is he checking up on me? I thought our date was tonight. I must look like a wet mop doll. My hair, my ugly knees… Ahhhh!*

Amy walked toward the edge of the crowd of players where Suzy stood smiling.

"Great goal. What is Colt doing here with his best buddy?" asked Suzy.

"I can't think about soccer. I feel like I'm standing bare-assed naked in front of him. How the heck should I know why he's here? I just wish he would go away." answered Amy as she tried to blend in with the crowd.

Suzy couldn't help smiling at the predicament her friend was in. She envied Amy who seemed to have everything.

"It's probably no big deal. Maybe he just wants to support you."

"Oh my gosh, isn't it time for the second half to start yet? Maybe he won't notice me if I'm at the other end of the field."

"There's no chance of that. You're one of the best soccer players in Western Washington. Everybody notices."

"Oh no, here he comes. Do something. Hide me."

As Colt and Bobby approached Suzy put her hand on Amy's shoulder.

"Too late, girl. Oh hi, Colt," said Suzy.

"Uh, hi Suzy. I just wanted to talk to Amy for a minute, okay?"

"Sure Colt. But you better go easy on her. I think she's in shock."

Colt looked at Amy. She now did not resemble the talented player who was on the field minutes ago.

"Hey, I'm sorry if I freaked you out. I just wanted to see how you play. Also, I'll be picking you up an hour earlier," said Colt.

A still stunned and distracted Amy replied, "Oh, okay. Five instead of six, then?"

"Yeah, I have a surprise for you. I'll see you then. I just wanted to say that you're really good. It makes me wish I was still playing when I watch."

Amy brightened and smiled. "Great, I better get on the field. I'll see you later."

"Bye," said Colt.

Amy watched Colt and Bobby walk toward the parking lot. She could see Bobby talking and gesturing to his friend.

"Man, is she good or what? Did you see that move? It's like a woman playing with girls. Don't let this one get away, Colt," said Bobby.

"I don't know that I have much to say about it, dude," said Colt.

~~~

Amy sat next to Colt in the front seat of his car. She looked stunning in a bright blue dress over sleek nylons and a trace of makeup. Her light brown hair was left to hang free and shone like satin. Colt was drawn to this beautiful girl in many ways. He hoped that his plan would make her happy. He hoped that it would bring them closer together.

"So, why won't you tell me where we're going? What's the big secret?" said Amy.

"I just want you to meet a few people. It shouldn't take long. Then we can go to the movie. By the way, you look really great," said Colt.

Amy hit Colt's arm a few times.

"I can't believe you snuck up on me today. I looked like a wet mop."

"You looked like a winner to me," said Colt with mock look of pain.

"Let me know next time. I'll remember not to show up."

Colt pulled over and said, "Here we are."

"But Colt, this is your house? Who's here?" aksed Amy.

"Come on. This will be fun."

Amy started to lean down to avoid whoever was opening the front door of the house when she saw Colt's sister, Kelly. The tall, poised young woman waved and smiled. Amy stopped worrying, forgot about Colt, jumped out of the car and walked toward the house. *I guess maybe this will work out okay,* thought Colt.

"He didn't tell you anything, did he? He wanted to see how you would do under pressure," smiled Kelly.

"Of course he didn't say anything. Our first date and he puts me on the spot. It's great to see you though. He was right in knowing that I would love to see you again," said Amy.

"Come on in. I asked Colt to bring you over. My mom wants to meet you, too. Don't worry. We can be friendly when we really try."

Leona soon joined Kelly and Amy in the living room. Colt decided to leave them to their girl talk and went to his room. Amy soon felt like part of the family with Kelly as a sister. Kelly was exactly what Amy aspired to be. She was a successful college soccer player and an excellent student. Kelly was also friendly, relaxed, and not caught up in her own success, which made everyone who met her feel at ease. The three women talked liked they had known each other for years until Colt interrupted them.

"Hey ladies, you've got five more minutes before we have to go."

"Okay, little bro," said Kelly.

"I'm glad Colt brought me by," said Amy.

"Remember that we have a scholarship for you if you decide not to go to Western," said Kelly.

Leona hugged Amy.

"It was great meeting you dear. Please encourage Colt to keep at the school work so he can get into college, too. Come back any time."

Colt started the car and was about to step on the gas when Amy stopped him.

"Wait a minute."

"Oh, what's up?" said Colt.

"I liked my surprise. Your family is really nice."

"Be happy you didn't meet the old man." said Colt with a smile.

Before Colt knew what was happening, Amy had leaned over, firmly grabbed his chin, and kissed him. Although he was a bit startled, he adjusted to this new turn of events and returned the passionate affection that he was receiving. Colt sensed that there was a deep connection between them that was now active and expanding. It was like a bolt of lightning in a bone-dry forest. A blaze of passion, both emotional and physical, exploded. It created a scintillating cocoon that surrounded the two teenagers. A delicate river of happiness flowed between them.

Chapter 24

------Email-------
From: Sweden, Ron[swedenr@yahoo.com]
To: Carbon, Matthew[MatthewC@hocs.biz]
Subject: Colt O'Brien needs our help

Hi Matthew

The O'Brien kid needs to get a certification more than anyone. It could be the difference between getting into college or not. Mr. Towne asked me to pay special attention to his progress. When he has his assessment I think we should all be there to support him.

Regards Ron

------Email-------

    Amy pushed away Colt's hands and looked at him with a mock serious stare.

    "I'm here to help you study and not to play around. I can't believe how hard this stuff is. I thought it would be like any other studying I've done, but it's not," she said.

    "I told you it was bad. See why I'd rather fool around?" asked Colt.

    "So far you're doing pretty good. A few more hours and I think you'll be ready for the test."

    "Really? I'm glad to hear someone say those words. It's been like running a marathon that never ends."

"I can see that you've been working at it. Let's keep going until I'm sure you know it."

Colt and Amy went back to focusing on the study materials instead of each other. Passing the exam was important to both of them.

Damn, I want to be at Western as much as she does. I wonder if she knows how hung up I'm on her, thought Colt. Their romantic attachment deepened daily. Both of them were in uncharted territory. Neither had felt the intensity they were experiencing now. Being together was intense and thrilling. Neither of them wanted to think about any possible problems. As it was, nothing between them was forced, uncomfortable or awkward, allowing them to bask in dreamy, carefree comfort. Neither could envision a future without this effortless bond.

The study regimen that they followed was simple. Amy asked questions and Colt answered. The questions were gleaned from the two books and printed practice tests that Colt had been studying. Colt was starting to understand how repetition solidified his understanding. What seemed impossible only weeks before now was absorbed, digested and understood. All through his school years, he rarely studied any subject or assignment more than twice. *Now I get it. It really does start to sink in, even if it seems like it will never happen*, he thought. The one area where he knew about repetition was sports. He recalled hours and hours of doing the same soccer drills until it was like breathing. Now that he had taken the same approach to studying, he could see that it had the same effect. The difference was that the work was mental and not physical. As it happened in sports, his potential was uncovered by pushing himself. *It's almost like cheating*, he thought.

"Okay, that's enough. When you can answer the question before I finish saying it, you're ready," said Amy.

"So, you think I can pass?" asked Colt.

"If you can't pass, then they changed what's in the test. You really know this stuff."

"This is great. So, now what do we do?"

Amy reached over and grabbed Colt's hands, pulling him toward her.

"Do what you were doing before we started."

~~~

Billy answered the ringing phone in his basement bedroom.
"Hi."

"This is Colt. I'm ready for the test. What do I have to do?"

"You'd better talk to my dad first. We usually do an assessment."

"What's that?" asked Colt hoping that it didn't involve more studying.

"We sit down and ask questions to be sure that you're ready." said Billy.

"Is your dad there?" asked Colt.

After a few moments Matthew came on the line.

"Hi, Colt. Billy said that you want to take the NT Workstation certification exam?"

"Yeah, I'm ready."

"We want to have you come over so we can assess your readiness and give you some tips."

"I'm not into it, but if you say so I'll do it. Can I bring my girlfriend along?"

"Sure, bring her. And tell her we'd love to have her try this out, too. How about Friday evening at seven?"

"Okay, we'll see you then," said Colt.

"You know, Colt, it would probably be better doing this at the Sweden's house. They have a big table we can all sit at."

"Whatever. I want this over with. We'll see you Friday."

~~~

Amy sat next to Colt at a large table in the dining room of the Sweden home. Mr. Sweden, Mr. Carbon, Billy and Gunnar sat across from them. An open laptop was on the table in front of Gunnar. Two tall stacks of books and a four-inch high stack of printouts were also there.

Mr. Carbon spoke first.

"It's great to see Amy here. We all want to encourage her to join the program and get a certification. It's something that could help her in the future. We need more women that understand technology in the workforce. There are tremendous opportunities for women right now."

"This is the assessment. It's the last step before taking an exam," said Mr. Sweden.

"What do I have to do? Man, you really have a huge pile of books and stuff sitting there."

"The basic idea is that we ask you questions from any of the materials that we use. It could be any part of a book or a practice test question."

"But I only read the two books," said Colt.

"If you know it, we'll be able to tell. We've done a few of these. No student has ever failed an exam after passing the assessment." answered Ron Sweden.

"Okay, I might as well give it a shot. Can Amy answer, too? We studied together."

"As long as you answer on your own," said Mr. Carbon.

Gunnar waved his hand to the adults. His father nodded to him.

"If you pass the assessment, then you can do cram week. You study really hard the week before the test."

"I feel like I just had months cramming. But I probably will want to study hard just before doing it." answered Colt

The adults sat and watched as Billy and Gunnar used almost all of the materials on the table to formulate a variety of questions. Some were short but many were convoluted and intricate. Colt asked for clarification when wrestling with some of the long scenario questions. Amy was pleased to see that Colt gained confidence as he became absorbed in the assessment. After about twenty minutes he started to answer all of the questions correctly with little hesitation.

"Ask Amy a few questions, too," said Mr. Carbon to Billy.

"Okay Dad."

Amy had attempted to answer the questions that Colt was asked, but not out loud. She had become focused and found herself in the zone as she and Colt liked to refer to it. When Billy asked questions, she pulled from knowledge gained working with Colt. She was surprised and pleased that she was able to give solid explanations for many of the questions that were asked. Although Amy had never considered learning about computers, she was encouraged by her success. After it was obvious that Amy knew much of the material, Mr. Carbon stopped his son.

"That's enough. Colt probably wants to know how he did." he said.

"Yeah, I do," said Colt.

"You and Amy go out on the porch. Give us about ten minutes.

With the pair gone, the group discussed the session.

"He's more ready than we were for our first test," said Billy.

"I think he could pass now with no problem, even without cram week," said Gunnar.

"Okay, it's settled then. What about Amy? I think with a little work she could pass, too," said Mr. Carbon.

"I think she's the reason that Colt knows the stuff," said Gunnar.

"Billy, go get them," said Mr. Carbon.

Amy and Colt walked out of the Sweden's smiling. As soon as Colt closed the door behind them, he turned and hugged Amy. She kissed him on the lips and hugged him tighter.

"Oh Colt, you were so great. You didn't miss anything."

"You were, too. You really helped me," said Colt.

"I know I helped a little but you did it on your own. I'm so proud of you," said Amy.

"Are you going to try to pass a test?"

"I might. Let's see how it goes with you first. Can we do the cram week together?" asked Amy.

"I sure hope so. You're my lucky charm. Let's go to Starbucks and celebrate," said Colt.

"Oh, I'm so excited for you. I'm so excited for us," said Amy.

Chapter 25

```
------Email-------
```
From: O'Brien, Colt[ColtOB@yahoo.com]
To: Jones, Bobby[Bobbyj@yahoo.com]
Subject: Good news
```
-----------------------------------------------------------------
```

Hey Dude
I got some good news. Let's talk. Call me and we can decide where.

Colt

```
------Email-------
```

Leona called to Colt from the kitchen in a singsong, happy voice.

"Honey, could you meet me in the living room, please."

"Yeah Mom, I'm coming," said Colt.

Colt plopped on the sofa facing his smiling mother. Leona walked over and hugged him with eyes closed. *Uh, something's up*, thought Colt.

"Don't forget your appointment with Dr. Sharman. It's important that you go."

"What was that for again? I feel fine," said Colt.

"Don't you remember? It's a physical exam. You need those every so often."

"I'm not really that into it. It's at four, right?" said Colt.

"Yes. His office is next to Highline Hospital. He moved about a year ago. Maybe he'll have a surprise for you." said Leona with a noticeable joy in her voice.

"Ooohh! What aren't you telling me?"

"I just have a feeling that you're very healthy. Now give me a kiss and go back to what you were doing."

"Okay, but I have a feeling you aren't telling me everything."

What is this about? At least it sounds like good news. I'm glad I won't have to wait long to find out.

This simple incident brought into focus how much Colt loved his mother. His inner self felt a delicate radiance surrounding him from Leona. Where he sensed that he could never live up to his father's expectations, he knew that his mother loved him without conditions or criticism.

I really lucked out. She's the best, he thought.

~~~

Colt sat in the waiting area of Dr. Sharman's office near Highline Hospital. He was restless and resented waiting. *Crap, this always happens. He takes forever. This is why I don't like coming.*

Colt looked at Beth, the receptionist behind the main desk.

"How long will it be, Beth? It's like he's always running late," said Colt in frustration.

At about 45 years old and having worked for doctors for many years, she had the look of a person who had seen it all. Still, her bright green eyes expressed friendliness and curiosity behind the reading glasses perched on her nose. She gave Colt an understanding look and spoke.

"I think another fifteen minutes or so. You know how he is."

"Man, I get really bored just sitting here."

"There are plenty of magazines there."

"Whatever," said Colt as he stood up and stretched.

"Oh, it looks like it's time to go in. Follow me," said Beth.

151

Colt followed her to the scale where she weighed him and measured his height. She smiled and took him to a room. The friendly woman walked with a light step that gave Colt a feeling of anticipation that he had no reason to feel. He sat in the antiseptic room staring at pictures of the human body on the wall. *Oh no, more waiting. This room is lifeless. And, I'm jacked up for some reason. Hurry up, doc.*

After about ten minutes Dr. Sharmen knocked on the door and entered. When he smiled, Colt forgot his irritation at having to wait and remembered how kind the he was.

"How is young Colt today?" asked the doctor.

"Hey, I feel great. Like a million bucks."

Colt knew that this doctor treated people and not symptoms. Once he was past the waiting, he always enjoyed the slow methodical pace. He felt pampered and valued. The kind man checked Colt's blood pressure. Next, he looked at Colt's heart and ears.

"Have you had any problems, Colt? Your mother told me that you were in a fight."

"No problems, doc. I healed up fine. I'm not even sure why I'm here," said Colt.

"It's good to come in at least once a year, but I have some good news for you."

"I knew something was going on the way my mom was acting. Well I like good news, so tell me what's happening."

"She asked me about the possibility of you growing taller, so the last time you were here I did some tests."

"Uh, really? I didn't even know what the heck you were doing. What did you find out?"

"Not only do the tests show that you should grow quite a bit more, but Beth told me you've grown two inches in the last six months. So, maybe you're in the middle of a growth spurt."

Colt jumped up out of his chair and started to do a little dance with his arms alternately rising toward the ceiling and coming back down to the ground. Doctor Sharman smiled and backed up a little to give Colt more space to express himself. He was happy to share in Colt's glee. After a few minutes, Colt stopped.

"This is awesome. How many more inches will I grow?"

"The tests indicate that you could be over six feet, but it's difficult to determine for sure."

"So, that's all I came for? I can go?" said Colt.

"Yes Colt, you can go. And congratulations," said Dr. Sharmen with a big smile.

Colt grinned while sitting in his car. Images flashed across his inner vision. He saw himself as a taller, more composed person. The new Colt would be very successful, a person in charge of things. People would look to him with respect and admiration. He knew that this one bit of news would change his life. *I knew I was never supposed to be a midget and I was right.*

~~~

Bobby Jones sat facing Colt in the Burien Starbucks. He looked uneasy. Colt knew that something was troubling his lifelong friend.

"Man, I never see you anymore. I'm still here, bud," said Bobby with a shrug.

"Dude, don't get bent out of shape. I'm here now. You know that I'm studying a lot and I have a girlfriend again. I haven't forgotten who my best friend is," said Colt.

"Yeah, but it's like you disappeared."

Bobby noticed that Colt seemed less frenetic and more composed. It reminded him of the purple house with the clouds when Colt went into a trance.

"It's all good. Great things are happening for me," said Colt.

"Well you look laid back, man, and happy."

"What's the best thing that could happen to me?"

"Passing a cert test? Getting married? Hell, I don't know," said Bobby.

Colt stood up and raised his hands in a victory stance.

"I've grown two inches and will keep on growing. I could be over six feet tall some day," yelled Colt.

The few customers in Starbucks looked up at the boisterous teenager and wondered if the coffee he was drinking was a bit strong.

After years of hearing Colt complain about being short, Bobby knew how important this event was to his friend. Bobby understood and shared in the joy that Colt felt. It was like a triumph over the odds for both of them. Bobby stood up and thrust his arms toward the ceiling and jumped right along with Colt. Both young men crowed like they had won a championship game after being extreme underdogs.

"Awesome, man, awesome," said Bobby.

Chapter 26

------Email-------
From: Strong, Amy[AmyS@aol.com]
To: Bower, Suzy[sbower@hhs.edu]
Subject: Colt

Suzy

You were right. He's the only one for me. I love him soooooo much.

Amy ♥♥♥♥

------Email-------

Colt knew that it must be a dream, but the scene before him seemed so real that it held his attention like a vise wrapped around his head. He sensed that it was a cold winter night, but he couldn't feel the elements. He was hovering in a vacuum with only memories to fill in the gaps that his senses could not. Below him was an empty, wet, soccer field. Huge blinding lights gave the ground a shiny, ice-like quality. Colt longed to be on that field with teammates and cheering fans. He wanted to feel the thrill of racing down the field toward the goal with the rain hitting his face. He remembered the total abandon of competition where everything was simple and pure. *Dude, you miss it. You really do miss it.*

A crack of thunder in the distance shook Colt away from his pleasant memories. He was puzzled. *Why did I hear that? It was quiet.* His attention turned to the direction of the sound. A raging storm was approaching. Angry, charcoal clouds were

155

highlighted by flashes of bright red light. With each thunder crack, he felt an electrical charge surge through him. He knew that this was no disinterested act of nature. He felt tremendous anger pummeling his soul. *That thing is coming for me. I have to get out of here. It will burn me up.*

The vicious storm was now in front of Colt, who was helpless to do anything. His mind and soul were overpowered with each electrical shock freezing him in place. Now, he saw only red and he felt only scathing, hot currents burning through him. He tried to scream, but no sound came out. He started to cartwheel. With each attempt to act he turned over and over, moving faster and faster. Very soon he lost his ability to think at all. Images started to come at him in rapid succession. Thousands of pictures hit him, as if an invisible fast forward switch had been pushed. His mother, father and sister flashed by. Sentences streamed at him. He saw Amy and Bobby. Thousands of computer screens filled with icons, pictures and menus came at him. When he had almost lost consciousness, it stopped. *Now what?* He first felt and then saw her. It was Alison Monroe. Her eyes were like those of a dead person and her face had a bright red glow. The only expression of life her face displayed was a large grin that formed a sneer. Colt felt like an enormous straw was attached to his chest and the zombie Alison Monroe was sucking all of the energy out of him. He accepted the inevitable death that would soon take him.

Then, he woke up.

~~~

Leona picked up the phone.
"Hi, this is Ali."
Leona smiled.

"Hi Ali. How are you doing?"

"I guess I'm okay. You know that things have been difficult for me."

"It's always bad when marriages don't work out. Maybe we should get together and try to forget about it. What do you think?"

"That's sweet of you to offer. What did you have in mind?"

"How about scones and tea here at the house? We can forget about men for awhile," said Leona.

"That would be perfect, really perfect," said Ali.

Leona felt more connected to Alison Monroe after Colt had fixed her computer. She was happy to help someone who was having a hard time. Now they could have a pleasant visit.

~~~

Colt and Amy had been studying for the upcoming certification exam in Colt's bedroom. He would take the exam in a few days and this was the final run toward the finish line. Colt was becoming very good at answering test questions and was becoming cocky. *This will be a snap. I even know the reason behind each question and answer. When I pass this thing a lot of doors will open for me.* He knew that understanding how computer networks functioned would create vast new possibilities. He smiled inwardly as he imagined himself strutting through this newfound world with all of the answers.

"Wow, this is fantastic. I know I can ace this test," said Colt.

"I think I can pass, too," said Amy.

Colt thought about their future, which seemed full of unlimited joy. *She really supports what I want to do.*

"We make a great team." said Colt.

Amy smiled and blushed. Nothing could make her happier than to hear those words.

"I love that we did this together, Colt. It brings us closer."

"I know how important it's been. You helping me, I mean. I feel like we can go up against anything that comes at us."

The two teenagers sat facing each other. A bubble of mixed emotions encompassed them. Feelings of love, desire, fear and nervousness moved into and out of the contained space they resided in. They sensed a connection that was more than infatuation. Both were uncomfortable with the intensity of their emotional bond. Colt closed his eyes and envisioned Amy holding his hand. They were looking over a cliff into a raging sea. He knew they would jump and it frightened him.

Amy said, "Sometimes, I get afraid. I don't know what I'd do if you weren't with me."

Colt was jolted by the statement. *Yeah, I feel the same. It's like the world would end if we weren't together.*

Just as Colt was leaning over to hug Amy, Leona called from the living room.

"Colt, Colt, come in here. Ali stopped by." said Leona

Colt had an instant reaction that centered in his gut and radiated out to his entire body. He felt like he'd been dropped from a moving car onto concrete and was bouncing in the middle of a highway. He was hit hard and could not recover his composure for a few minutes.

"I'm in the middle of something, Mom."

"Honey, come in and say hello. It won't take long."

Amy could feel a change in the connection that she and Colt shared. It was like static had blurred the clear channel that ran between them. She became afraid as they neared the living room where the older women sat. As soon as Alison Monroe looked at Colt, a dark feeling of dread came into Amy. *Why do I feel this way? I don't even know this woman,* she thought.

Colt surveyed the two women facing him. One he loved and one he now feared. He could see that his mother was not aware of anything off-key. She was anticipating a pleasant exchange between friends. Ali looked at Colt. He remembered his dream and said nothing only nodding and showing a brief smile. Her face was rather blank and seemed indifferent toward him or Amy.

"Hello Colt," she said.

When she spoke, Colt recognized the spark of desire in her voice and the need for revenge deep within her eyes. He was sure that Amy had seen it, too. He knew that this meeting would end badly.

"Uh, hi Alison," Colt replied.

"You know you can call me Ali, Colt."

Now, even Leona could sense that something was not right. The tension between Ali and Colt was increasing by the second. Just when Colt was turning to get away, Alison Monroe started to cry. In a few seconds large tears were rolling down her cheeks. She was also moaning loudly between convulsions. *I knew this was going to be bad. I guess I should have known she would do something weird. But why did Amy have to be here?*

"Oh no, what's wrong, Ali. What's wrong?" said Leona.

"I thought I could come here and it would be okay," cried Ali.

"What do you mean? What are you talking about?"

She pointed to Colt, who was frozen like an icicle. *Oh no. Not with Amy here. No, no!*

"I mean him."

"What about him?" asked Leona who was now feeling her maternal instincts rising up.

"I thought a glass of wine would be okay. But, but he kept pouring and drinking, and pouring and drinking. Then he used me; he screwed and used me. I'm so ashamed. I just wanted my computer fixed and he took my self-respect away."

Colt looked at his mother who was stunned, but had a look of determination. She glanced at Colt with mixture of hate and disgust on her face and turned back to Ali, who was now trying not to smirk. Colt was starting to think that this might be the first time his mother stopped loving him. She then surprised everyone in the room. Leona O'Brien turned, snarled at the unsuspecting Ali Monroe and with clenched fist hit her, using every ounce of weight in her tiny body. A loud crack rang through the air.

Colt was stunned as his sweet mother started to yell at Ali Monroe. It was like a tornado had been unleashed and Ali Monroe was a house made of straw.

"You better not say another word about my son or I'll break your neck. I know that my Colt never took advantage of anyone."

Alison was now crying real tears of real pain. Her hand was on her jaw and her eyes expressed shock and fear. She backed away from Leona, who looked like she might pounce at any moment.

"But, but…." whined Alison.

"Shut up you bitch and get out! Get out!" yelled Leona.

Ali Monroe grabbed her purse and ran for the door. Colt could now feel Amy hitting his arm. She was wailing like someone had died. Colt sensed the snapping of the invisible cord that held them together. It was like a part of his soul was cut out by a dull, rusty blade. He felt like he was falling into a black pit that had no bottom. Amy pulled away from him and slumped down in a corner of the room sobbing.

It won't matter what I do. None of it will make a difference. I'll never be able to fix this, thought Colt. He waited until Ali was gone and then slowly walked toward the front door. He turned to look back. Both Amy and Leona were still crying. After seeing Amy, the little hope he nurtured vanished. Tears began to flow before he reached his car.

Chapter 27

```
------Email-------
From: Sweden, Ron[swedenr@yahoo.com]
To: Carbon, Matthew[MatthewC@hocs.biz]
Subject: Colt O'Brien
-------------------------------------------------------------------
```

Hi Matthew

I have been hearing rumors about Colt O'Brien. It has to do with a friend of his mother's. I will see what I can find out. I don't want our program to be put into a negative light.

Ron

```
------Email-------
```

Ron Sweden sat in his sedan in front of Highline High School with his cell phone glued to his ear. He was dressed, as usual, in a tailored suit that was spotless. It was a dreary January day; gray, drizzly and cold. His face displayed an expression of seriousness and curiosity. He cringed slightly, composed himself and spoke.

"Hello, this is Ron Sweden. I'm trying to get in touch with Alison Monroe."

"This is Alison. What do you want?" said a wary voice.

"I work with Highline students in a new certification program. It's a special computer networking course. Colt O'Brien is a student in our program. I've heard upsetting things about Colt that concern you. Before we kick him out of the program, I need to find out what happened. I was hoping you could tell me your side of what took place."

Ali perked up at the sound of 'kick out'. She was very angry about being hit in the face at Colt's house and wanted him to pay.

"Sure, let's talk, Ron. How about right now? Do you know where I live?"

"If you give me your address, I'm sure I can find it. I just happen to be available. So, now will be fine."

After giving Ron her address she said, "Thanks for listening to my side of the story, Ron."

"We want to know the truth about our students. This program sets the bar very high." he replied.

"I'll see you soon then," said Ali whose day was brightening by the minute.

Ron set his phone down and grabbed a small notepad from his briefcase. He concentrated and wrote *Alison Monroe - ????????*

We'll see how innocent this woman is, he thought.

In a short time, Ron Sweden parked in front of Alison Monroe's small house in Normandy Park. Although he wanted to keep an open mind, he already felt that Colt had been taken advantage of. His experience with all types of people was vast and he sensed that Alison had character issues. And, he had gotten to know Colt who he felt was not devious at all. With Colt it was 'what you see is what you get'.

After sitting down in the living room, Ron looked at Alison Monroe. He had declined her offer of white wine. He tried to act friendly, while secretly hoping to find the truth about what really happened between an 18-year-old young man and a thirty-something woman. Ron smiled and started asking questions.

"It is so nice to be able to talk to you. I feel that you must have been taken advantage of. So what happened?"

163

Alison took a large gulp of her wine, emptying the glass.

"He kept pouring the wine and telling me to drink it. Then no matter what I said, he wouldn't stop coming at me." slurred Alison.

"Oh, so he brought the wine with him?" said Ron.

"No, of course not. Oh, that reminds me. I think I'll have some more wine."

After refilling her glass and weaving her way back into the living room with a half-full bottle, Alison continued.

"I was sad and lonely. He used me."

"So, you told him to stop? You became intoxicated, but made it clear to him that you didn't want it to go any further?"

She thought for a while with her eyes looking off to a faraway place finding it difficult to focus.

"Well, um, er, yeah. That's the way it was," she mumbled.

So far, this woman has no credibility, thought Ron.

"One last question. Did Colt ever bother you after that? Did he stop by or call?"

Alison, who was overcome with emotion along with the effects of the wine, started to cry. After a few minutes she looked at Ron Sweden. Any pretense of calm was gone. Her makeup was running down her red face as tears continued to gush.

"No, my baby never called me. He doesn't love me. He screwed me and used me, and threw me away," sobbed Alison.

Ron Sweden was not able to hide his look of sad disdain, but Alison was too caught up in her emotions to notice. He stood, turned and left closing the door silently behind him.

~~~

After the visit from Ali Monroe, Colt understood his dream vision with the life force being sucked out of him with a straw. He felt heartsick and empty at seeing his mother and Amy so upset. *Crap, I sure ended up in a bad place. At least my Mom still loves me. But Amy... I just don't know.* He hoped that the broken relationship with Amy could be made right again, but became nervous whenever he thought about her. The anticipated certification exam was the next day, but it seemed less important now that Amy was not sharing it with him. As far as his mother's reaction to the visit, Leona never expressed any doubt about Colt's innocence. She talked to Colt the next day.

"Colt, honey. I'm so sorry I sent you over there to see that horrible woman. I should have remembered that recently divorced women can do crazy things. Now, let's forget about it and get you back together with Amy."

"Thanks mom. I know you love me."

However, Amy would not answer his calls or emails. *Man, I could pass this test and still my life might be crap.* Colt felt relieved that Bobby would go with him to Wings Aloft for the test. *I need someone I trust there with me. It's like everything got screwed up. And, who else has Ali told her lies to?* Having the support of his friend would be a great comfort. Now that Colt was down, he appreciated Bobby as never before.

Colt sat facing his computer in his bedroom with a phone to his ear.

"Hey Bobinator."

"Hey man. How are things? I'm sure glad I don't have your kinds of problems," said Bobby.

"Yeah, things are messed up. Let's meet. We can talk or whatever."

"How about lunch at Dave's Diner at one?"

"Sure thing, dude. Later."

165

Colt walked out of his house and toward his purple car. When he was a few feet away from the vehicle, he noticed a run-down truck parked across the street. He thought he could see somebody behind the dingy windows, but couldn't be sure. *I wonder why that's parked there? Oh well probably no big deal.* As he reached his car, Colt turned to open the door. A swoosh of air hit the back of his neck causing him to turn. Everything he remembered after that was disjointed and painful.

Two medium-sized young men dressed in ratty clothes with numerous tattoos and spiked, colored hair, grabbed Colt. In one swift movement, they slammed the door with his hand still attached and pounded his head into the side of the car. He had no chance to defend himself or even cry out. The rough attackers let him go and he fell to the pavement, stunned and helpless. His left eye was already bleeding and needles of excruciating pain were throbbing through his right hand. One thug pinned Colt to the ground while the other kicked him in the side and yelled over and over again, "Remember Ali Monroe, punk." When he started to slip into darkness, he felt his attackers loosen their grip. He had no sense of who or where he was. From the end of a tunnel that seemed far, far away, he heard a voice say, "Run, before I kill you."

~~~

Colt awoke to the sound of steady rain. It was dark outside and he had no idea of the time. His body was filled with excruciating pain. The pain was everywhere. His left side, right hand and eye were a bit more noticable, but it was difficult to distinguish any location that was more painful than any other. Colt groaned and soon the door opened. His father and Bobby walked in.

"Colt, are you still alive? Do you even remember us taking you to the emergency room?" asked Bobby.

With great effort, Colt raised his throbbing head.

"Huh? Where? Dude, what happened?" asked Colt.

"Your dad said some ugly goons were pounding on you when he pulled up. He chased them away." answered Bobby.

Robert O'Brien looked at his son with worry, which made Colt think that he must really look as bad as he felt.

"Colt, here is some aspirin and an ice pack. The doc said you would be okay, but you need lots of rest. Your mother can't bear to look at you. I think the blood and bruises are too much for her," said Robert.

"Thanks Dad. After the incident the other day, she's probably wondering what will happen next."

Though things were still a bit hazy, Colt thought he saw his father wink at him and smile.

"Your mother told me she took care of that woman. From what I heard, Ms. Monroe tried to ambush you. I think she sent those punks, too. Anybody that would do that can't be a good person." said Robert O'Brien.

"I hope Mom is okay," said Colt.

"She's more afraid than anything. She saw how you looked when I brought you in. As far as your girl, I expect that the real truth will come out and she'll hear it. It usually does," said Robert.

"I feel like crap and I have my test tomorrow," moaned Colt.

"Mr. Sweden called about that. He said that it would be good if you could make it, something about a scholarship."

Colt did not answer as he slipped into a painful unsettled sleep.

Chapter 28

------Email-------
From: Wise, Deborah[DebbieW@aol.com]
To: O'brien, Leona[LeonaB@aol.com]
Subject: She's a horrible person

Dear Leona

I heard about your son being hurt by those thugs. I know for a fact that Ali seduced Colt. He was innocent. After she poured wine down his throat it was easy to get him to do what she wanted. I think the breakup made her a little crazy. But having Colt beat up because he broke it off is more than I can take. She has turned into a horrible person. I just thought you should know the truth. Please call me if you want to talk more. I hope Colt is ok.

Debbie

------Email-------

Delicate rays of winter sunlight poured into Colt's bedroom, forcing him to lift his heavy eyelids. His beaten body shouted out. Swelling pain assaulted him. At seeing a stack of books, he was jolted into remembering what he needed to do. His mind tried to change gears, but his weakened body refused to follow. *Damn it. The test is today. What a hassle this is going to be.* Dizziness hit him when he attempted to sit up, forcing him to pause for a few moments. *Whoaaa. I better move slower. I need something to kill this pain.* Colt trudged toward the kitchen with a bottle of aspirin in his hand. *At least I smell coffee.* Leona was on her way out the front door and Colt paused to avoid seeing her. He was relieved that no one would be in the house to see him weak and bruised.

After taking four aspirin and drinking strong coffee, Colt sat in the living room. He brought his focus back to the certification test he was supposed to take that day. He knew that taking the test would be challenging in his present condition. Still, he pictured a series of steps leading to success. His psychic vision indicated to him that he had to pass the test today for the dominoes to fall according to plan. With renewed energy he dialed his friend's number.

"Yo, Bobster," said Colt.

"Hey Man, how are you doing? You sound bad."

"Dude, I feel like I was beat up by some mean, ugly dudes, but I'm starting to move a little."

"Are you still doing the test thing?"

"Yeah, I have to play through the pain. I need to do this," said Colt.

"What's the plan, then?" asked Bobby.

"Pick me up at 11:00. The test is at 1:00. We can get some lattes or something."

"Man, are you sure? I can't believe you're even getting out of bed."

"Dude, just be here," said Colt with more conviction than he really felt.

Colt tried to relax and conserve his strength. Although he thought that studying would be good, he feared that using up what little energy he had could be disastrous. *I better just chill until the test.*

Bobby pulled up in front of the O'Brien home. Colt hobbled out of the front door. To Bobby, he seemed to be moving in slow motion. He was wearing a lime green parka, aqua-colored pants and high-top pink tennis shoes. Large, dark sunglasses covered some of his bruises, but not all. Under his arm he carried one book and a thick stack of printed test questions.

"Where to?" asked Bobby.

"Let's go to Starbucks. I'm not into food right now."

"Good idea. I'll buy. You deserve something. Man, I still can't believe you're doing this. You look just as bad as I thought you would."

"I just want to get it over with and then crawl into a hole for a week."

After the coffee stop, the young men drove to Wings Aloft. During the drive, Colt attempted to focus on the task ahead with less than optimal results. His friend tried to cheer him up by saying anything that he thought would be encouraging. Colt entered a neutral, semi-meditative state in order to hold onto the little energy he had. It was laborious work to maintain even minimal focus, but he hoped that he would stay cognizant enough to pass the test. *Man, I didn't know how bad I was. I can't even think straight. This would've been easy, but now it'll be hard to just function.* Colt started to become upset, but stopped himself. He knew that a state of frustration would sap the little strength he possessed. *I have to watch out or I'll be useless before long. And I thought this would be easy.*

The two young men entered the Wings Aloft training center. Colt was surprised at the large front room with floor to ceiling windows. He saw Billy and Gunnar with their fathers sitting in a corner. The group seemed small to him in the cavernous room. Colt had removed his sunglasses and his injuries were now in plain view.

"Wow, are you okay?" asked Gunnar.

"I'll live. I need to get this test done," said Colt.

Mr. Carbon spoke. "You don't have to do this now. You can reschedule."

"Thanks, but the hard part was getting here. Now that I made it, let's do this."

"All right, Colt. Come over to the table and the boys will go over some things," said Mr. Carbon.

Colt tried to listen as Billy and Gunnar gave him tips on how to approach the exam questions. They emphasized staying calm and not being overwhelmed by the fact that it was the real thing. Because of the throbbing pain, Colt didn't grasp much of what the well-intentioned boys were saying. However, to his astonishment, one tip was very clear to him. It was something that would usually not seem important, but now seemed especially helpful to Colt.

Billy was speaking.

"I try to get a song going in my head. It helps me get into a rhythm. I think that's the whole trick to this. You need to get into the zone. We all study so much that it's not if we know it, but if we relax."

After listening to the boys, Colt signed in at the front desk. The tall, blonde, twenty-something girl told him that he was not allowed to carry any notes or electronic devices into the test room.

"No problem. I'll leave my stuff out here. I guess you know the rules. What's your name?" said Colt.

A slight sparkle flashed across her eyes.

"I'm Greta. I already know your name," she said. "It's a little early, but I can take you up now if you want."

"The sooner, the better, Greta. I'm ready."

The kind lady gritted her teeth with concern.

"Are you okay?"

Colt grimaced when answering.

"Uh, yeah, I think I'm okay. I've been asked that a lot today."

After receiving encouraging words from the boys and their fathers, Colt looked at Bobby. He came to Colt's side and put his arm gently around his shoulder.

"Hey man, I know you can beat this bad boy. Just remember, it's pass or fail. Don't worry about getting every question right," said his friend.

"Thanks Bud. I'll see you on the other side," smiled Colt.

Tall blonde Greta led Colt outside to the two-story building where he would take the exam. She walked up the stairs with Colt behind. At the halfway point, Colt felt throbbing, dizzying pain and stopped to regain his equilibrium. Greta turned at the top and looked back at Colt, who was grabbing the railing. Her face was pale with fear. After what seemed to both of them to be hours rather than minutes, Colt continued up. At the top of the stairs Greta held the door open. Colt felt a strong urge to leave. As his mind created numerous, logical reasons why he should not attempt to take the exam, his legs dragged him forward. Before he could turn around, he was in.

Chapter 29

------Email-------
From: Bower, Suzy[sbower@hhs.edu]
To: Strong, Amy[AmyS@aol.com]
Subject: Find out the truth

Hi Amy
Before you send Colt to hell for hurting you, find out
what really happened. I hear rumors that it wasn't just
Colt messing up here.

Your Friend SusyQ

------Email-------

Colt looked around the empty exam room. It was no more than a cubicle with two personal computers and a telephone. The silence was thick and Colt could hear his own scattered thoughts bouncing around inside his throbbing head. The pulsating pain and an increasing ringing in his ears made Colt feel unfocused and angry. *Crap, this is like being in a coffin. If the walls were any closer I'd choke to death.*

He read the instructions on the computer screen and began. After reading the first question, which was long and tiring, the throbbing pain increased along with the scattering of his thought waves. He was tempted to click on an answer without re-reading the question or looking at the detail of the possible answers. *Damn, these answers all look the same and are really long too. If they're all like this I'll never finish.* Colt took his time and eventually decided on the answer he wanted. However, when he tried to move the mouse, his beaten hand ached along with his head. After switching the mouse to the other hand, he marked the question and continued. The next question was short and he recognized the answer immediately, which raised his hopes but did not lessen the effects of his injuries. *Maybe I can get through this after all. If half of the questions are like this, I should be okay.* The next three questions were similar to the first in complexity and length. Colt became frustrated and angry. He had now completed five questions, but could only be sure that one was correct. As he read the other questions again and again, he became more confused. *Damn it all. I'll never be able to do this.* He feared that his ability to perform was lost in the pain of his battered body and might not return, at least not today. In his mind a large black clock with glowing yellow dials was hovering over his head ticking away the seconds and minutes.

Colt stopped to gain his composure. *I'm not in the zone they talk about. I don't even feel close to being in the zone. I don't even remember what a zone is.* A sense of failure assaulted him. He thought of Amy and the mess with Alison Monroe. He thought about a future of failure and mediocrity. *I can't even get past the first thing.* The foundational building blocks that he had expected to fall into place were now transformed into nondescript buildings being blasted apart by a nuclear explosion. A bleak world remained; a science fiction world of devastation and emptiness.

As Colt began to feel faint and dizzy, he raised a hand to his head with eyes closed. He saw red flashes of lightening in black storm clouds. *Hmmm, where have I seen those before?* He knew that he was supposed to be focusing on something, but he couldn't remember what that something was. The red storm came at him and the ringing in his ears became a vibrating roar. As he tried to escape from the angry storm, he found refuge in a pleasant humming sound that calmed him. *That's better. Sooo peaceful.* The still roaring wind was not as pronounced and the humming sound had taken on a melodic quality. As he vibrated with the humming sound, Colt became merged with the storm that had now transformed into an ethereal wind. He was uplifted and pulled along in a universal current. His mind no longer functioned in the usual way. Everything seemed so far beneath him, so far behind him.

Colt floated and floated, not knowing where he was or where he was going to. Time was no longer something that bore down upon him, but a wisp of a memory. The storm of hatred was gone. The ethereal sky that he now inhabited was serene and joyous. Nothing could penetrate this new sublime world. As he adjusted to this new experience, Colt's inner eyes began to open. He could make out the colors white and blue with a hint of purple. The indistinct colors were gently massaging and healing him. When he surrendered to the feeling of serenity and peace, he realized that he was seeing clouds. They were light, fluffy, billowing, but most of all, friendly clouds. He knew he had been in those clouds before, but that exact memory was not with him now. It was another memory of a distant, forgotten place that had no hold over him.

In this new place, everything seemed so natural to Colt. He didn't worry about recent events or the test while hovering in the ethereal cloud bank. His attention was slowly pulled toward a hazy white glow. For a brief moment it seemed like something he should remember, but he forgot why. As he turned toward the glow it became brilliant, blinding him. He absorbed this new experience without emotional reaction or conscious thought. He was a sponge for the light coming toward him. Again, he automatically adjusted and by doing so, allowed himself to merge with the light.

What had been overpowering incandescence now became individual beams of pure white light that emanated from an angelic face. It was an ageless face, a woman's face. As she came into focus, he could feel her personality and thoughts. Her blue eyes were like the depths of the sea. They penetrated into his soul with love and playfulness. Her bright, scintillating hair sparked with ever-changing crimson flashes. The vibrating, emanating light made her cream-colored face seem reflective of an inner sun.

As he became accustomed to the blanket of distinct rays, Colt connected to the angelic being like high branches on a tree connecting with its own roots. In an instant, he digested the imprinted thoughts that the angelic woman was transmitting to him. There was no conscious thinking, but an understanding in a deeper part of him. The experience was of enormous impact, but had a light, matter-of-fact feel to it.

Although Colt had traveled far away from what was known to him, he knew that the arc of his journey was a boomerang back to himself. As he began to feel a shift to that other familiar place, he could hear music and words. They guided him and imbued him with a sense of lightness akin to the place he was leaving. He recognized the song as "Take Me Home" by Phil Collins. The music never sounded so good.

Chapter 30

```
------Email-------
```
From: O'Brien, Leona[LeonaB@aol.com]
To: Wise, Deborah[DebbieW@aol.com]
Subject: Thanks
```
--------------------------------------------------------------------
```

Debbie
I'm so happy we talked. I didn't know how messed up
Ali was. That woman is poison to my Son. I feel like I'm
partially responsible for asking him to go over to her
house. And, he tried to break it off without causing any
problems. I just love him that much more. I think I
know how I can make it up to him

Thanks again
Leona

```
------Email-------
```

Colt was sitting cross-legged in the middle of the small exam
room. Dreamlike memories danced in his head along with
words and music from the Phil Collins song, "Take Me Home".
I guess I know what an out-of-body experience is, but I wonder who that
woman was. And that music. Where did that come from? He smiled,
still feeling a joyous glow. *I guess I won't have enough time to finish the*
test after all of that. Whatever, I gave it a shot. An inner sense nudged
him, but he took little notice. The pain from his injuries had
subsided. His mind felt un-cluttered and razor-sharp. As he
looked at the computer screen, he noticed a timer in the lower

177

left corner. It displayed "1 hour 58 minutes remaining in this exam". *Wow, that can't be true. It felt like I was gone for hours.*

The next exam question beckoned to Colt, who did not feel that it mattered if he passed, failed or even finished. At the same time the music and words to the song became more prominent. It was as if as if the song, which was very clear, was a river carrying him along on a lazy day. Everything seemed so unimportant now. His encounter with the angelic woman made him feel that he was connected to a benign universe, that his life was destined to come out alright. He didn't feel a sense of urgency about anything. In his mind, the exam mattered little in the grand scheme of things. *Whatever, Dude. The world will keep spinning.* Still, the feeling that he should continue answering questions became stronger and the music changed into a tidal wave that pushed him forward.

As if talking to an overbearing parent, he said aloud, "Okay, okay, I'm doing it even if it doesn't matter."

Then, something occurred that startled Colt. So far his experience, as different as it was, had felt like a dream and it was difficult for him to see it as anything else. Now in a waking state, he heard something that validated what had happened to him. A woman's voice came to him. It was an audible, melodic whisper.

The clear, feminine voice said with conviction, "Listen to the music and finish what you came here to do."

He obeyed without question. Colt was surprised when he saw how obvious the answer to the question displayed on the screen was. The next question was longer and had five possible answers that were almost identical. As Colt became frustrated, the music soothed him. After a brief internal struggle, Colt became calm and analytical. He re-read the question and carefully read all five answers. He saw that two answers were incorrect, which narrowed the possible answers to three. After looking at the three remaining answers, he noticed that two of the questions had identical words, but the order was reversed. He eliminated the third remaining answer from his mental list. Now, Colt paused to reflect. He knew something had changed within himself and that it was a permanent change. *I'm not the same. That going into the light thing made me different.* Processing the test questions had become easy. Most of all, he had a logical system to decipher the questions, which gave him an optimal chance of providing the correct response. And the music in his head provided a rhythm that became an internal compass, aiding in his ability to focus. *Yeah baby. Now, I'm in the zone. I'm really in the zone.*

Colt moved through the remainder of the exam with ease. He remembered playing soccer; how natural and enjoyable it had been. As if he was playing a sport again, Colt flowed through the exam without straining. At times, he moved fast, but when necessary slowed to fully comprehend a question. To Colt, he was competing again, which made him feel confident and fulfilled. When he reached the end of the exam, he returned to the four marked questions. Two were correct and two were incorrect. He didn't question how he knew if an answer was right or wrong. It was obvious to him now.

The music inside Colt's head stopped. *That must mean I'm done.* After he clicked on a button with the words "End Exam", a screen displayed a complete list of all questions. After verifying that he had not skipped any questions, he clicked again to continue. In the middle of the screen at the left he saw the word "pass" and beneath the word "fail". Before he knew what had happened, a horizontal green bar flashed across the screen. There were numbers above it, designating the percentage of correct answers. He had been confident and expected a good score, but was not prepared for what he saw.

As Colt walked toward the door, a dizzy feeling came over him. His body felt like it had been bounced around in an empty cement mixer. *Uh, oh. Here we go again. I should have known this great feeling wouldn't last.* It was fortunate that there was a railing at the top of the outside stairs. He held on as the world spun around him, trying to find an anchor point. After a few seconds, Colt was able to steady himself enough to look down to the wet asphalt below. What he saw did not make sense to him. There were at least thirty people looking up with anticipation. He wondered why they were there. *Are they waiting for me?*

A familiar voice shouted up to him, "Well, did you pass?"

Colt recognized his father's voice, but still did not realize why he was there. As he tried to remember what he was there for, all the events of the day flooded into his head. Trying to make sense of everything, he was overwhelmed. It was as if his mind was a small cup overflowing with an ocean of experiences. When he started to feel like he was about to go over a raging waterfall, he saw the crimson-haired angel lady. She was smiling at him.

"I got them all. I got them all," he said.

Colt felt a firm hand grab his arm as he slipped into darkness.

Chapter 31

------Email-------
From: O'Brien, Kelly[Kellyobrien@UW.edu]
To: Strong, Amy[amystrong@aol.com]
Subject: Let's talk

Amy
Let's talk. I know you were hurt by what happened with Ali Monroe. It wasn't really Colt's fault. And it was before you guys started going out. Our whole family would really like you to be at the celebration of Colt's getting the certification. Why don't you come over to the house for a visit?

Kelly

------Email-------

It was Saturday morning. The entire family would be attending the victory celebration in honor of the certification program, in general, and Colt in particular. Colt sat on the couch in front of the TV, channel-hopping while Leona made breakfast in the kitchen. Pleasant aromas wafted throughout the kitchen and living room. The smell of coffee, bacon, eggs and toast caused Colt's stomach to growl. He turned around and craned his head to look into the kitchen. *Man, isn't it ready yet? I'm starved.* His sister, Kelly, was helping her mother. Having a big event for just passing a test seemed like overkill to Colt, but he was now a believer in the leadership of the program. Every time he had expressed doubts about why things were done, he ended up being wrong. If there was a party, he would be there.

It had been a week since the exam and Colt felt great. His wounds had healed but he was still trying to understand what had happened during the exam. Many questions remained but the happiness of that day still was present. Much of what occurred was difficult for him to comprehend and some parts seemed so other-worldly that he did not trust that it had been real at all. It was still difficult to understand why he was able to perform so well on the exam. It all seemed so real, but he could not find a way to incorporate the experience into his young mind. However, as much as he wanted to deny that any of the more esoteric parts were real, he had an unshakable, positive sense that the universe was a wonderful place. His self-esteem remained consistently high with an inner compass resolutely pointing toward success and growth. The only vexing thing in his life was that he had not been contacted by Amy. He thought about her constantly. *I know one thing. Nothing is the same, no matter what I try to tell myself. I can't get pissed off about anything, even if I want to.*

After Leona called the family into the dining room, they all began to eat. Colt attacked the eggs, and fried potatoes that overflowed his plate. As he took a sip of dark coffee, he saw that his mother's eyes were starting to glisten.

"I know we don't eat together as a family very often anymore. I'm so happy on this wonderful day that we could all be here," said Leona.

"This is great, Mom. You too, Sis," said Colt.

Tears of joy were now streaming down Leona's face as she waved both of her hands. She quickly gave up the losing battle of holding back the tears.

"I wasn't going to cry, but I can't help it. Your father has something to say, Colt," said Leona.

"Son, your mother and I are very proud of you. I've talked to various individuals about this program you're in and I saw firsthand that it works. It's great that you joined and made the commitment. Everybody can see the obstacles you overcame to pass that exam and earn the certification. We think that you made a huge step toward securing a bright future with the effort you put in."

"Thanks Dad. I feel like it has changed me for the better," said Colt.

"And that whole business with my ex-friend, Ali Monroe, is over. We know you were falsely accused," said Leona with a fierce look in her eyes.

Colt thought he saw his father wink behind a brief smirk. He felt that he had connected with his dad at last. Whether it was passing the exam or the incident with the older woman was a mystery, but he didn't care.

Man, it's like a miracle. The old man knows who I am.

Although he had stopped looking to his father for fulfillment, he couldn't ignore the new bond that he felt. Colt sensed that a missing piece in his life was now in place.

A light knock came at the front door. Colt thought, *who could that be?* His father rose and went to the door while the two women smiled. In a few moments, Colt's heart stopped beating and hope sprung up like wildflowers after a drought.

Amy Strong walked over and hugged Kelly, who was now standing. Amy was wearing a white chiffon blouse with a gray skirt. Nylons below and pearls above gave her a sophisticated appearance. Her satin brown hair was hanging down around her shoulders. To Colt, she looked stunning. He started to become misty-eyed himself.

Amy looked at Leona and Robert.

"Thank you for inviting me. Through everything, I've always felt that I was a part of this family," she said.

"You always will be, dear," said Leona.

When she turned to Colt he was speechless. He felt that an inner vacuum was being filled with fresh scented oxygen. Amy seemed to him like a beautiful princess who was too royal to be approached. Then, he thought about all of the experiences that he wanted to share with her as he could with no one else.

"I guess we haven't talked in a while," said Amy. "Let's go into the other room and catch up."

Wow, thought Colt.

~~~

Ron Sweden stood at the podium in the Highline High library. There were about forty adults and teenagers in the audience. The crowd went silent as he started to speak.

"Thank you all for coming. We're here to recognize the achievements of young students doing extraordinary things. We started with two dads and two kids. Now all of you are involved, or will be soon."

He continued speaking about the program and its success for about ten minutes, all the time slipping in positive references to Highline High School and the school district. He never pointed to the founders as the reason for success but the audience knew where credit was deserved.

"Now, I would like to call Mr. Towne up to say a few words. He's been a supporter of the program, from the beginning."

The short, energetic Highline principal walked rapidly to the stage. As he turned to the audience, all were drawn in by his radiant enthusiasm. The respected man spoke.

"Thank you, Ron. I'm so proud of what has been accomplished by all of the students. We're now going to open up this program for more young people. This approach is different than what we have done in the past, but we're seeing great results. No student is a better example of what this program is about than Colt O'Brien. I encouraged him to participate. He could have taken an easier road, but he chose to face the challenge, to be an achiever. I was there when he passed his exam. He was in great pain, but refused to use that as an excuse. I saw him collapse into his father's arms after he finished with a perfect score. I have a special award to present to Colt for setting an example for others to see. Colt, please come up here."

Colt said a few words of thanks and allowed the applause to wash over him. *I guess it is all worth it.*

After the speeches, Colt, Amy and Bobby stood together as Colt was congratulated by a continuous parade of parents, school officials, and students. Billy Carbon and Gunnar Sweden strolled up, bringing a smile to Colt's face.

"Dude, the little nerds are here. When I got into this thing, I thought you guys were full of it. Now I know both of you are for real. Thanks man. I know you guys are always going to make good things happen."

"Thanks Colt. You showed us something at the test. Man, we thought you were going to die," said an awestruck Gunnar.

"Yeah, we still don't know how you could concentrate on those questions when you were so beat up," said Billy.

"I had a lot of help from guys like you and Amy. I guess I couldn't forget the stuff," said Colt.

Mr. Towne walked up with an older man at his side. He was tall with white hair that made him seem very distinguished.

"Hi, Mr. Towne," said Colt.

"Hello, Colt. This is John Warner. He's from Western Washington University," said Mr. Towne.

"Hi. Mr. Warner. This is Amy Strong and Bobby Jones. They've both been accepted at Western already. I applied, but haven't heard back yet." said Colt.

John Warner offered his hand, which Colt shook.

"That's why I'm here, Colt. We've looked at your grades and your other accomplishments. I came here with an offer for you," Mr. Warner said.

"Oh? An offer? What is it?" asked Colt.

"Like any large university, we have an extensive computer network. It's difficult to find experienced students to help us keep it up and running smoothly. I'm authorized to offer you a full scholarship to Western if you'll be a member of our networking group while you attend. So, think it over and let me know if you're interested."

"I don't need to think it over, Mr. Warner. Count me in. And thank you."

"I'll get you all the information through Mr. Towne. He represented you well in our discussions."

Colt looked at Mr. Towne, who was beaming.

"Thanks Mr. Towne. I appreciate everything you've done."

Mr. Towne put an arm around Colt and shook his hand.

"That's what we do here, Colt. We help young people reach their potential."

On the way home, Bobby drove with Colt in the front seat and Amy in the back.

"I'm starting to get tired. Whew! What a day. Before I forget, I want to thank you guys. You both have always been there for me. I'm happy you're both here with me today," said Colt.

"Hey, man. You keep us guessin', Colt," said Bobby.

Amy leaned into the front seat and kissed Colt firmly on the lips, and did not pull away for a long, long time.

Chapter 32

------Email-------
From: O'Brien, Robert[ROBrian@aol.com]
To: Norman, Ted[TNorman@yahoo.com]
Subject: Colt

Hello Ted

Many good things are happening with my son Colt. After not achieving very much, he caught fire and is now catching up with his sister.
You may have heard rumors about Colt and an older woman. I'll tell you this. I am going to make sure that her life becomes very unpleasant.

Robert

------Email-------

Colt sat in his father's black Lexus in the pouring rain wondering why he was there. He liked that his relationship with his father had improved but still fell into his old habit of expecting the worst when they were together. *I have to remember that it's not like it was. Dude, the old man has changed. Trust a little.*

As they pulled out of the driveway of their Normandy Park home, Colt still had no idea of where they were going.

"Uh Dad, where are we headed to?" asked Colt.

"I thought we could have a boys' day out. We can get some coffee at Starbucks and then I have something to show you," answered Robert.

Colt always looked forward to a Starbucks visit and felt like it was a comfortable place for the two to talk. *This might be okay.*

~~~

In another part of Normandy Park gusting wind carried large raindrops that pelted Alison Monroe's' small house. Alison sat in her living room staring out of the large picture window in deep thought. A large mug of coffee sat on the table.

After the unsuccessful visit to Colt's house and the talk with Ron Sweden had not had the desired effect, she felt that drastic measures had to be taken. Extreme emotions, fueled by white wine and stronger alcohol, had led her to hire the thugs that assaulted Colt. That part had been easy. Her friend John Haydon, who had a somewhat suspect past, had supplied the two hoodlums to do the deed and had even paid them the money for her.

Now that she had exacted her revenge, she knew that she needed to move on. Pangs of desire and regret still arose but she sensed that any more contact with Colt would be wasted effort. Although she had no fear of being punished for her actions, she didn't want to put herself at risk by continuing on her present course. She quit drinking altogether and kept a low profile. Her alcohol replacement was strong coffee and menthol cigarettes. She also decided to start seeing John Haydon to help her forget about Colt. He turned out to be less exciting as a boyfriend than he had been as her ally. However, she felt safe having him around.

A knock came on the door. Ali answered and let in her boyfriend John. He was about 40 years old and thin with dark hair. He hadn't shaved in a few days and smelled of marijuana and cigarettes.

"When is this god-awful rain going to stop?" he said as he sat down.

Ali again wondered why she picked him to be with.

"So let's talk about the thing with Colt O'Brien." said Ali.

"How many times to we need to go over it? Nothing's going to happen. The guys you hired are laying low. It's all good." answered John in a frustrated tone.

"I want that part of my life to be over with. I want to go on without any worries."

"Are you starting to feel guilty about it?"

"He deserved everything he got and more. I just wish I could have been there to see it," scowled Ali.

John moved next to her and kissed her on the cheek. She lightly pushed his hand away. He leaned a bit harder and put a hand on her thigh. She stared with irritation as she removed his hand. After waiting for a positive response from her, John stood up and spoke.

"You don't seem that friendly today."

"I have a lot on my mind. I think it would be better if I was alone."

He thought about his options and decided his best one was to leave. He could feel tension building and wasn't in the mood for a fight. He had seen what happened when her temper flared and he wanted no part of it.

"Uh okay. I'll take off. I'll call you later." he said as he kissed her goodbye.

Ali didn't answer but lit a cigarette and went back to staring out of the window. Before she could find the train of thought that she was looking for a knock came on the door.

"What the hell, I just got rid of him," she whispered in frustration.

She opened the door to see John Haydon, sopping wet and looking like a trapped animal. As he walked in she noticed a man in a suit behind him.

"I'm with the Burien Police Department. Are you Alison Monroe?" asked the man.

She considered slamming the door and stopped herself.

"Uh, yes that's me." she answered.

"I'll have to ask you to come down to the station for questioning. We have two men in custody who are accused of a felony."

"Why are you asking me to come with you? Am I accused of something?"

"So far you haven't been charged with anything but if you don't clear this up, you could be soon. Mr. Haydon has decided to cooperate since he's on parole and could go back to prison. So what do you say? Will you come in?

Alison Monroe was so angry that she slapped John Haydon across the face. He didn't respond except to look down.

"Hell no, I'm not going with you. I haven't done anything. You can talk to my lawyer." she yelled.

"Ms. Monroe, I'll ignore that slap but expect to see me again very soon. Goodbye for now." said the officer.

A sleek black automobile was parked across the street from Alison Monroe's house. The rain had let up a little allowing a clear view for Colt and Robert O'Brien who sat inside. Both smiled as Robert's friend Christian Ames walked a handcuffed John Haydon toward his car.

"It won't be long before everybody has talked and Alison Monroe is in custody too." said Robert.

"Thanks Dad. This is awesome. You sure know how to surprise a guy."

Just then Ali opened the door and peeked out. Robert started the Lexus and put it in gear while rolling down the window. He waved at the sobbing woman as they drove away.

Chapter 33

------Email-------
From: O'Brien, Colt[ColtOB@yahoo.com]
To: Jones, Bobby[bobbyj@yahoo.com]
Subject: One more thing

Hey Dude

Life is good. My girl is back. I made it into school. The test thing was hard but I like it when I'm getting somewhere. I have one thing I want to do. Call me.

Colt

------Email-------

The day was overcast and rainy. The rain was more than a sprinkle, but less than a downpour. Although it was about one in the afternoon, very little sunlight was seeping through the clouds. The purple VW bug sped away from downtown Burien toward the Puget Sound with Colt behind the wheel and Bobby sitting next to him.

"Where are we going? What's the big secret?" asked Bobby.

"It won't take long. You'll know soon," said Colt.

In a few minutes they parked in front of the Carbon's house. As the friends walked up the driveway they both were surprised that the lilac colored building did not have the same intense effect as it had before. The two young men could see a small woman sitting in a chair behind the front picture window when they walked to the door. After knocking, Billy Carbon answered.

"Is your dad here?" asked Colt.

"Hi guys. Come in. My dad went to the store. He'll be back in a few. We can wait downstairs," said Billy.

As they walked into the front room toward the door to the basement, both Bobby and Colt looked at the living room and the petite lady who was sitting in the large chair with a book in her lap.

"Oh, Mom, this is Colt O'Brien and Bobby Jones. They came to see Dad. We told you about Colt and his test," said Billy.

She looked at both young men with a pleasant, knowing smile and said "Yes, I remember. I believe I talked to Colt on the phone briefly. Please sit down and we can talk while you boys wait."

After settling into the plush antique couch, both boys had a chance to look at Elyce Carbon. She seemed to be perfectly matched to the room that she was sitting in, with its antique furniture and prints. Colt was distracted by the clouds painted on the ceiling and didn't look directly at his hostess. He could feel a lessening of tension with each deep breath that he inhaled.

"I heard that the exam was very challenging for you, Colt. Everyone was very impressed with your courage," said Elyce.

Colt was stupefied when he heard her voice. He felt as if music had filled his body. It was powerful, colorful music. Then he remembered the song that he heard during the exam. He looked toward the person behind the words and was stunned. Although she looked somewhat different, Colt knew he was looking at the same angelic woman that was in his vision. The red hair was not as red and the blue eyes were not as blue, but her aura was the same. She wore blue jeans and a bright purple blouse on a body that did not weigh more than 95 pounds. In his mind, he could only see the angel woman of his vision.

No doubt it's her. What does it mean?

Colt tried to focus but could not remove the powerful vision of light that he experienced on the day of the exam.

"It was hard. I was in a lot of pain and I saw some stuff that was sort of weird," he said.

She smiled and both young men could feel a delicate, penetrating radiance coming into them.

"I've heard that stress can make people experience many unusual things. Was it like a dream?"

"Yes, it was sort of like a dream, but I wasn't asleep," said Colt.

"I certainly hope that the waking dream was not too distracting. I heard you passed the exam, so it must have been your way of dealing with the stress."

"I passed and I don't even know how," answered Colt.

"Well, it's good that it all worked out. Don't worry too much about the unusual things. Sometimes, unexplainable things happen to people. I have to go now. It was nice talking to you both."

She stood up and walked by the boys toward the stairs going to the top floor. As she passed, her arm brushed against Colt. He felt like he was transported back into his vision from the exam. Unspoken words came to him in her melodic voice. *Do not be afraid of your special talents. You will be led to do great things if you have faith in yourself.*

Colt smiled, jumped up, and said, "Dude, let's hit the road. We can talk to Mr. Carbon later. We have stuff to do."

About The Author

George Matthew Cole lives in Burien, Washington with his wife and dog. After a long career in the computer support field, he became interested in writing. The idea for "Colt O'Brien Sees The Light" came from personal experience working with high school students over a two year period.

Find more information about the author
and his books at his web site.

www.georgemcole.com.

NOTE FROM GEORGE MATTHEW COLE

After reading "Colt O'Brien Grows Up" please take a little time to write a review and submit it to the bookseller of your choice. Written reviews are important to the author and potential readers, as well. The review can be as little as a few sentences or much longer. It's really up to you. I hope you will enjoy my book but, even if you don't, please write a review.

Thanks George

Also by George Matthew Cole

Colt O'Brien Grows Up
El Porto Summer

Made in the USA
Lexington, KY
11 November 2016